In Captain Picard's office, Admiral Jellico was making no attempt to hide his astonishment. He said again, "Calhoun? You don't mean Mackenzie Calhoun?"

"I most certainly do," said Picard, unflappably sipping his tea. "He was simply a damned fine officer. One of the best we ever turned out. And he's right for this command." He began to tick off reasons on his fingers. "He knows that region of space. His home world, Xenex, is right up against the Thallonian frontier. If the Thallonian Empire is falling apart, you're talking about planets at war with each other. Angry factions at every turn. We need someone who can pull worlds together. We need Calhoun's strength and skill now more than ever before."

"He's unpredictable," Jellico said.

"So are the circumstances. They'd be well suited."

"He's a maverick. He's a troublemaker. He's—"

"In this unique situation, the challenges it presents . . . Calhoun is the best candidate."

"You're trying to put a cowboy in the captain's chair," Admiral Jellico said.

"Absolutely," Captain Picard replied. "After all, this is a new frontier."

STAR TREK®
NEW FRONTIER

BOOK ONE

HOUSE OF CARDS

PETER DAVID

POCKET BOOKS

New York   London   Toronto   Sydney   Tokyo   Singapore

An *Original* Publication of POCKET BOOKS

POCKET BOOKS, a division of Simon & Schuster Inc.
1230 Avenue of the Americas, New York, NY 10020

A VIACOM COMPANY

This book is published by Pocket Books, a division of Simon & Schuster Inc., under exclusive license from Paramount Pictures.

ISBN: 0-671-01395-5

First Pocket Books printing July 1997

10 9 8 7 6 5 4 3 2 1

Printed in the U.S.A.

To The Fans . . .
You Know Who You Are

Editor's Acknowledgment

I would like to thank Paula Block for her help in turning *New Frontier* into a reality, Peter David for the fantastic new characters he peopled the *New Frontier* with, and Gene Roddenberry, whose sandbox we're playing in.

—John J. Ordover,
Senior Editor

TWENTY
YEARS
EARLIER . . .

M'K'N'ZY

I.

FALKAR REGARDED THE REMAINS of his troops and, as the blazing Xenex sun beat down upon them, decided to wax philosophical about the situation. "It is not uncommon to desire killing a teenager," he said. "However, it is not often that one feels the need to send soldiers to do the job."

His men regarded him with a surprising amount of good cheer. It was surprising they had any left, for the battle between themselves and the Xenexians had not only been brutal, but also extremely unsatisfying. Although not particularly unsatisfying for the Xenexians.

They were a somewhat bedraggled lot, these survivors. Their armor, their clothing, hung in tatters. Their weapons were largely energy-depleted, and when they had fled the scene of their final rout, they had done so depending heavily on short swords and knives to hack their way to safety (or what passed for safety). Weapons that hung at their sides largely for ornamentation, for decoration, for a symbol of achievement. Most of them had never touched the bladed weapons except to polish them for display purposes. Not one man in fifty could remotely consider himself expert with their use. As Falkar studied the barely two dozen men remaining to him, it was as if he could read what was going through their minds.

Falkar drew himself to his full height, and as he was six and a half feet tall, there was something to be said for that. His skin was a dark bronze, as was that of all the people of his race. His build was an interesting combination of both muscle and economy. There was no denying the power in his frame, but it stretched across his body in such an even manner that—despite his impressive height—it was easy to underestimate just how strong he was. His hair was long and black, and usually was tied neatly, but now it hung loosely around his shoulders in disarray. When one is beating a hasty retreat, it's hard to pay attention to keeping one's hair properly coiffed.

His eyes were solid black, his nose was wide and flared, and his incisors were particularly sharp.

"Perhaps we deserved our fate," he said tightly.

His men looked up at him in surprise. If these were words meant to comfort an already dispirited band, they were not doing the job.

"We have ruled the Xenexians for over three

hundred years," he said tightly. "Never, in all that time, has there been any uprising that we were unable to quash. Never has our authority been questioned. And because of that, we have allowed ourselves to become sloppy. Become overdependent on hand weapons." He was striding back and forth in front of his troops. "We came to believe," he continued, "that we would be able to win battle upon battle, not because we were the better prepared or the better armed . . . but simply because we were *entitled* to do so, as if by divine right. Well, the Xenexians showed us differently, didn't they?"

"It was that damned boy," one of the soldiers muttered.

Falkar spun and faced him, his dark eyes glittering. "Yes," he said, voice hissing tightly from between his teeth. "That damned boy. That *damned* boy. The one who rallied his people. The one who outthought us at every turn. The one who anticipated our moves, who was not intimidated by us, who gave his people hope. *Hope,* gentlemen. The worst thing people such as these could have. Because hope leads to action, and actions lead to consequences. And the consequence of these actions is that we are now faced with a people who stand on the brink of liberation. We fight them and fight them, and they keep coming back and defeating us. Our government, gentlemen, has made it clear to me that they are beginning to consider Xenex more trouble than it is worth. And that damned boy is the cause."

Falkar had been standing on the uppermost reaches of a plateau. Now he pointed out at the formidable terrain before them. It stretched on for hundreds of miles, seemingly in every direction. The ground was hard and cracked. Small mountains dotted the landscape, and there were small bits of vegetation here and there clinging desperately for life.

"He's out there, gentlemen. Out there in the Pit. Providence has potentially put him within our reach. His vehicle was seen spiraling out of control in that direction during the battle's waning moments. He's separated from his troops, from his followers. He is alone. He is no doubt scared. But he is also very likely dangerous, as would be any trapped and injured animal." Falkar turned and looked back at his men. "I want him. Alive, if possible. Dead, if not. But if you capture him alive and he 'accidentally' meets his demise in transit, make certain that all injuries he sustains are to his body. I want his face pristine and uninjured, easy to identify."

One of his soldiers frowned. "I don't understand, sir. Certainly he could be identified from DNA records in any event."

"True," said Falkar. "But I'm referring to being able to identify his face . . . when his head is stuck upon a pole in the great square of Xenex." He surveyed the terrain one more time and then said, "Find him. Find M'k'n'zy . . . and let's put an end to this rebellion once and for all."

M'k'n'zy felt his left arm stiffening up again. The blood that covered his biceps had long since dried; the large piece of metal that had embedded itself in his arm had cut him rather severely, and it had been a hellish few minutes to pry it out of where it had lodged itself. That wasn't the major problem though. The big difficulty was that he had dislocated the damned limb. The pain had been excruciating as M'k'n'zy had braced himself and, agonizingly, shoved it back into place. It had been so overwhelming, in fact, that M'k'n'zy had fainted dead away. When he came to a few minutes later, he cursed himself for his weakness.

He treasured the small bit of shade that he'd managed to find for himself as he extended his fingers and flexed them, curved them into a fist and straightened them once more. "Come on," he muttered to himself through cracked lips, expressing annoyance with the uncooperative portions of his body. "Come on." He worked the fingers, the wrist, and the elbow until he was satisfied with the movement in them. Then he surveyed the territory, trying to assess his situation.

While Falkar was wild of mien by the moment and by happenstance, M'k'n'zy had that look to him all the time. His skin also had a burnished look to it, but had more of a leathery texture to it than Falkar's, most likely due to the fact that he spent so much time out in the sun. His hair was wild and unkempt. The Xenexians had a reputation for being a savage people, but one look into M'k'n'zy's purple eyes bespoke volumes of intelligence, cunning, and canniness. No one who thought him a simple scrapper could hold to that opinion if they looked into his face for more than a moment.

One would never have thought that M'k'n'zy was merely nineteen. The years of hardship he had endured gave him a weathered look, with several deep creases already lining his forehead. And more . . . there was something in his eyes. Whatever innocence he had once possessed was long gone.

Those savage eyes scanned that section of Xenex called the Pit. It was an area approximately thirty miles across that was well known to the people of M'k'n'zy's home city of Calhoun as someplace from which people should—under ordinary circumstances—steer clear. For starters, it was extremely inhospitable, filled with small life-forms that had developed various nasty abilities required for surviving in the desert environment. Moreover, the weather was severely unpredictable, thanks to a combination of assorted fronts which would slip in and become trapped within the mountains that ringed portions of the terrain. Fierce dust storms would whip up at any time, or torrents of rain would fall—sometimes for days—to be followed by such calm and dryness that one would think that there had been no precipitation there for ages. In some areas the terrain was cracked and dry, while in others the ground was exceedingly malleable.

Beyond the physical challenges the place presented, there was something else about the area as well. Something that bordered on the supernatural. Those who were advocates of pseudoscience would claim that the Pit was a source for a rift in reality. That it was a sort of nexus, an intersection for multiple realities that would drift in and out as easily as dust motes caught up in vagrant breezes. Those who were not of a pseudoscientific bent just figured the place was haunted.

Either way, it was the most unpredictable piece of real estate on Xenex.

But although modern Xenexians gave the Pit a wide berth, centuries previously it had been part of a fundamental rite of passage among Xenexian youth. When a Xenexian reached a certain age, he or she would trudge into the midst of the Pit to embark on what was called the "Search for Allways." It was believed that, if one wandered the Pit for a sufficiently long enough time, visions of one's future would reveal themselves and one would come to understand one's true purpose in life.

However, the Search for Allways began to take a significant death toll as young Xenexians would fall prey to the dangers that the Pit presented. As a consequence, the Search disappeared from the practiced traditions of the Xenexians. This did not mean, however, that it vanished from practice altogether. Instead, it went underground. A sort of dare, a test of one's bravery and character . . . and, if truth be told, ego. Those who felt that they had a destiny—whatever that might be—would take it upon themselves to embark on a Search of their very own. Parents would try to emphasize to their children the folly of such actions, just as their parents had before them. And in most cases they were no more successful in dissuading their own children than their own parents had been in discouraging them.

By the time M'k'n'zy was thirteen, he had no parents who could try and talk sense into him (although, to be fair, even if his parents had been alive, the odds are that they would have not been successful). Loudly proclaiming to his peers that he was a young man of destiny, M'k'n'zy set out for the Pit to discover just what that glorious future might be. As the (unofficial) tradition dictated, he went out into the Pit with no supplies save for a supply of water that would last him—under ordinary circumstances—one day.

Even with rationing, by the fifth day he had used up the entire supply.

It was day eight when his big brother D'ndai found him, unconscious, dehydrated, and muttering to himself. D'ndai brought him home and, when M'k'n'zy was fully recovered, he told his friends of the remarkable visions he had seen. Visions of his people free from Danterian rule. Visions of a proud and noble people rising up against their oppressors. And he recounted these visions with such force, such conviction, and such belief that they were attainable goals, that it became the basis for the eventual uprising of the Xenexian people.

The truth was, he hadn't seen a damned thing.

It was his great frustration, his great shame. It was the last thing he wanted to admit. And so, when his friends had pressed him for details of what—if anything—he had seen, he began to string together a series of fabrications which grew with every retelling. In fact, somewhere along the way even M'k'n'zy allowed himself to believe that his claims were reality.

Deep within him he knew this wasn't the case. But, like most men of destiny, he wasn't going to allow trivialities such as truth to stand in his way.

The Danteri made their way slowly through the Pit's northwest corridor. They moved with caution, surveying literally every foot of land before them. All of them knew that the Pit could be merciless on anyone who didn't keep his guard up at all times.

Falkar kept a wary eye on the skies overhead, trying to be alert to any sudden change in the weather. He'd never actually explored the Pit, but its reputation was formidable.

Falkar's aide, Delina, suddenly stiffened as he studied the readings from a sensor device. "What is it?" Falkar demanded.

Delina turned and looked at his superior with a grim smile. "We've got him," he said. He tapped the sensor readings. "He's stationary, approximately one hundred yards west."

"He's not moving?"

"Not at all."

Falkar frowned at hearing that. "I don't like the sound of it. He could be sitting there, knowing we're looking for him, trying to lure us into a trap."

"But isn't it just as likely, sir," suggested Delina, "that he's injured? Helpless? That he's resting in hopes of remaining in hiding? How does he even know he's being pursued, sir?"

Thoughtfully, Falkar stroked his chin and stared in the direction that the sensor indicated. Stared with such intensity that one would have thought he could actually see M'k'n'zy with unaided gaze. "He knows, Delina."

"With all respect, sir, you don't know that for sure. . . ."

Falkar fixed his gaze on Delina. "When our troops moved in for the surprise raid on Calhoun . . . he knew, and the city's defenses repelled us. When we were positive that we had them cornered in the Plains of Seanwin . . . he knew, outflanked us, and obliterated five squadrons. When my top advisors assured me that the Battle of Condacin could not possibly be anticipated, that it was—in fact—the preeminent military strike of the century . . ."

Delina's face darkened. "My brother died at Condacin."

"I know," said Falkar. "And the reason was that M'k'n'zy knew. I don't know how. Maybe he trucks with the spirit world. Maybe he's psychic. All that matters is that he knew then, and he knows now."

"Let him," said Delina fiercely. "Let him for all the good it will do him. If you'll allow me, sir, I'll rip his heart out with my own hands."

Falkar studied him appraisingly. "Very well."

"Thank you, sir." Delina snapped off a smart-looking salute.

With confidence, the Danteri headed after their prey.

The confidence lasted until they moved through a narrow passageway that led to the hiding place of

M'k'n'zy. Then there was a faint rumble from overhead, which quickly became far more than faint. They looked up just in time to see a massive landslide of rocks cascading toward them. There was a mad scramble forward as they tried to avoid the trap. Screeches were truncated as soldiers disappeared beneath the heavy stones. There was a brief moment of hesitation as the Danteri tried to decide—with death raining down around them—whether they should advance or fall back. Falkar was shouting orders, but was having trouble making himself heard above the din.

Falkar, in turn, did not hear Delina's shout of warning. All he knew was that suddenly Delina slammed into him, knocking him back against a wall. For a split second his breeding objected strenuously to such handling, but it was only a split second that he felt that way. Because a moment later the boulder that would have struck Falkar instead landed squarely on Delina, who hadn't been able to get himself out of the way in time. Delina vanished under the boulder, wearing an expression of both outrage . . . and satisfaction.

All of it happened within seconds. Ultimately the Danteri overcame their hesitation and did indeed drive forward, or at least the handful of survivors did.

They plunged headlong to safety, or so they thought.

In fact, what they plunged headlong into was ground that gave way beneath their feet. Falkar, bringing up the rear, stopped himself barely in time as he heard the alarmed howls from his men. The rumbling of the rockslide behind him was fading. On hands and knees, Falkar slowly edged forward and peered into the hole. Far below he saw the glint of some sort of underground cavern, and the broken bodies of his men down there. He glanced back over his shoulder and saw assorted hands and feet sticking out from between the rocks from the avalanche.

"Bastard," he hissed between clenched teeth.

M'k'n'zy mentally patted himself on the back. He could not have picked a better spot for an ambush. In the week he'd spent in his futile (and yet, curiously, productive) Search for Allways, he'd familiarized himself with much of the Pit. When he'd taken refuge there now, he had done so knowing that he was capable of outthinking and outmaneuvering anyone who might be so foolish as to try and chase him down. A simple, small explosive charge which he'd detonated from hiding was more than enough to do the job of bringing the rocks down.

As for the hidden cavern, M'k'n'zy himself had almost fallen victim to it several years previously. Fortunately he had, of course, been alone, so his far lesser weight resulted in only one leg going through the insubstantial covering above the caves. It had scared the hell out of him when it happened, but a scare was all it had been.

For the warriors who had been pursuing him, however, it had been a good deal more lethal.

Still, caution was called for. He had no intention

of making the same sort of foolish mistake that his opponents had made.

M'k'n'zy left the hiding place that he'd staked out in the upper reaches of the passageway and slowly made his way to where he could see the devastation. He peered down; thirty feet below, there didn't seem to be anyone moving. There were limbs protruding from beneath rocks, and farther beyond, there was the massive hole through which the remaining soldiers had fallen.

He nodded approvingly, but decided that it would probably be wiser to maintain altitude where he could. The high ground was always preferable, after all.

So M'k'n'zy began to make his way back to his home, back to Calhoun. He wondered what sort of reception would be there for him. He further wondered—hoped, prayed—that the Danteri had finally had enough. That this latest and greatest defeat had finally convinced them that the Xenexians would never give up, never surrender, never stop believing in the rightness of their cause. Sooner or later, the Danteri would have to get the message. If it took repeated pounding in of that message, then so be it.

He sniffed a change in the air around him, and he definitely didn't like it. He had the hideous feeling that a storm was beginning to brew, and he knew from firsthand experience just how quickly such things could come up. There were outcroppings of rocks around him, plenty of places where he could anchor himself and not risk being carried away by the fierce winds that a typical Pit storm generated. As a matter of fact, he had passed what seemed to be a particularly likely sheltered area only minutes before. Smarter to retrace his steps and secure himself there until the storm had passed.

He turned around and, sensing danger, came within a millimeter of losing his life.

The blade was right at his face. It had been sweeping around, aiming toward his neck. If he hadn't unexpectedly turned at that very moment, the blade would have severed the jugular vein. As it was, he reacted just barely quickly enough to survive as the gleaming blade sliced across his face, from right temple down across his cheek, down to the bone. Blood fountained out across the right half of his face as M'k'n'zy backpedaled frantically. But with him blinded by his blood, with pain exploding in his mind, the ground went out from under the normally surefooted M'k'n'zy. He fell, landing badly and aggravating further the already existing injuries to his arms.

And during all that, not a sound escaped from his lips.

"No cry of pain," Falkar said, pausing to survey his handiwork. As an afterthought, he wiped the blade of his short sword on his garment. "I am impressed, young man. As impressed, I should hope, as you are by my ability to have crept up on you without you hearing. What with your being a savage and all, I'd think you'd pride yourself on your instincts and ability not to be surprised. So . . . were you surprised by being surprised?" he added, unable to keep the smugness from his voice.

M'k'n'zy didn't say anything. He was too busy denying his deep urge to scream. He fought for control, breathing steadily, pushing away the agony that was eating away at him, dulling his senses, making it impossible for him to concentrate on the simple business of staying alive. His right hand was slick with blood; he was literally holding his face together.

"Did I take the eye out?" asked Falkar, in no hurry to finish the job. He had suffered far too many losses at the hands of this young twerp. In a way, he was glad that he had missed the initial killing stroke. That had been generated as a result of rage and—he hated to admit it—a tinge of fear in facing this crafty killer man-to-man. This way was better, though. Worthier. It was the best of both worlds, really: he could face his victim, and at the same time, not worry about him. "Perhaps I'll take the other as well. I could give you that intriguing choice. Kill you . . . or leave you, but alive and blind."

Truthfully, there was so much blood, so much pain, that M'k'n'zy couldn't even tell if he'd lost the eye altogether. His red-coated hand was clasped over the right side of his face. He felt himself dangerously close to succumbing to the ungodly torment that threatened to paralyze him. And he also knew that there was no way, despite what Falkar had just said, that Falkar was going to leave him alive. Oh, he might blind him first. Watch his progress with sadistic amusement and then kill him. Desperate for time, M'k'n'zy said, "I have . . . no love for my eyes."

"Indeed?" said Falkar. The steadiness of M'k'n'zy's voice was slightly disconcerting to him. "And why is that?"

And M'k'n'zy started to talk. Every word out of his mouth felt thick and forced, but he spoke and kept speaking to focus himself, to stave off the pain, to buy time . . . maybe even to remind himself that he was still alive.

"These eyes," he said, "in their youth . . . saw rebel leaders punished by having their unborn children . . . ripped from the wombs of their mothers. They've seen villages burned to the ground. They've . . . they've seen 'criminals' convicted of minor crimes . . . punished by having limbs lasered off . . . one at a time, screaming for mercy . . . receiving none. . . . They've seen my . . . my father tortured in the public square, punished for crimes against the state . . . a punishment ordered by you, you bastard . . . my father, beaten and whipped until a once proud man . . . was reduced to screaming even in anticipation of the blows. . . . They . . . they saw the look of pure shock on his face . . . just before his mighty heart gave out in the midst of the beating. . . . The last thing my father ever heard . . . was my begging him not to leave me . . . begging for a promise he couldn't keep. . . ." His voice choked as he said, "These eyes . . . have seen the hand of tyranny . . . and before I grew to manhood, I wanted to lop that hand off at the wrist. . . ."

M'k'n'zy's words made Falkar exceedingly nervous. Despite M'k'n'zy's continued ability to out-think and out scheme Falkar's own war chieftains, he had always harbored the image of M'k'n'zy as a grunting savage, operating mostly out of luck and a native wit beyond anything his fellow tribesmen might possess.

But what he had just heard was hardly the speech of a barely articulate savage. What the hell kind of person was capable of sounding erudite while losing blood out of his face by the pint? Suddenly all thoughts of toying with his victim, all intentions of dragging things out, evaporated. He just wanted this . . . this freak of nature dead, that was all. Dead and gone, and his head as a trophy.

What Falkar had not realized, however, was that M'k'n'zy's little speech served one additional purpose: a stall for time that allowed the coming storm to arrive. The storm that M'k'n'zy had sensed, which Falkar was oblivious of. But he was not oblivious any longer when the full blast of the storm abruptly swept down upon them.

It roared across the near plain, up through the canyons, and hammered down around M'k'n'zy and Falkar just as Falkar was advancing on M'k'n'zy to carve him to pieces. The wind was howling around Falkar, and he had no idea which way to look. Without having any time to prepare for it at all, Falkar was suddenly at the heart of a whirlwind. He staggered, buffeted by the powerful forces around him, and insanely he actually tried hacking at it with his sword. The wind, in turn, knocked the sword away from him. He heard it clatter away, turned in the direction that he thought it had fallen, but wasn't able to track it. Instead he found himself helplessly staggering around, unable to seek it out. He snarled *"I hate this planet!"* under his breath, and at that moment came to the conclusion that the Xenexians were welcome to the damned place. If he never saw it again after this day, he would count himself fortunate.

He couldn't see anything. He went to one knee, squinted fiercely, and bowed his head against the blasting of the wind. He felt around, hoping against hope that he would be able to locate his weapon. He'd probably have to track down M'k'n'zy all over again, because certainly the little barbarian would use this convenient cover to escape. That was the problem with Xenex: Nothing on the planet was ever simple.

And then wonderfully, miraculously, his questing hands discovered his fallen weapon. As the wind shrieked around him, his fingers brushed against the unmistakable metal of the blade as it lay on the ground. He let out an exclamation of joy and tried to reach over for the hilt so he could pick it up.

Suddenly the blade was lifted off the ground and for a moment he thought that the wind had tauntingly snatched it away once again. He lunged after it . . .

. . . and suddenly found that it was buried in his chest, up to the hilt.

And there was a mouth speaking softly in his ear, a nearness that almost seemed to imply a degree of intimacy. A voice that whispered, "Looking for this?"

Falkar tried to reply, but all he managed to get out was a sort of truncated gurgle. The sound of the storm diminished, replaced by a pounding in his head that blotted out all other noise. And then he rolled over onto his back, and the last thought on his mind was—unsurprisingly—the same thought he'd had only moments earlier. . . .

I hate this planet. . . .

II.

TRYING NOT TO THINK about what he was doing . . .
trying not to let the pain overwhelm him
completely . . . M'k'n'zy held his face together until
he was reasonably sure that blood was no longer
fountaining from the gaping wound. He had no idea
just how temporary the stoppage was. He was certain that the only thing preventing more bleeding
was the pressure that he was applying, and considering the fact that he was fighting off unconsciousness,
he had no clue how long he could continue to apply
that pressure. He had visions of slumping over and
bleeding to death through his sliced-open face.

He wondered if he would dream in that state. He
wondered what he would dream of. Would his father
and mother come walking out of swirling mists,
extend a welcoming hand to him and bring him to

wherever it was their souls resided (as the priests of Calhoun preached)? Or would there be blackness and oblivion (as M'k'n'zy suspected)? Then he realized his thoughts were drifting and he forced himself to focus once more.

The storm had begun to subside, and M'k'n'zy began rummaging around Falkar's body, using one hand while continuing to apply pressure to his face with the other. He was reasonably sure by this point that his right eye was intact, if for no other reason than that he didn't think anything was oozing out of the socket. But he could still barely see worth a damn, and he was operating more on feel than on sight.

He had already stuck Falkar's sword into his own belt. He felt the ornate hilt, and decided it was so elaborate that it was probably connected somehow to the royal house from which Falkar hailed. He checked around Falkar's belt and discovered some sort of pouch attached to it. He pulled on it, and it refused to yield. He yanked again, this time channeling some of the pain he was fighting off into the motion, and the pouch obediently came free. He rummaged through the pouch, hoping to find something along the lines of a first-aid kit. But there was nothing like that. Instead it appeared to be a tool pouch of some sort. Not unusual even though someone of Falkar's rank could hardly be considered a common repairman. Danteri prided themselves on being prepared for all manner of situations, and being able to make quick fixes would certainly fall under that consideration.

Then his fingers curled around something that he immediately realized could very well be of use. It was a small laser welder, handy for repairing any cracked metal surface (such as, for instance, a broken sword, or perhaps a vehicle with a hole torn in the side).

It was not, of course, intended for flesh. Unfortunately, that was the use that M'k'n'zy intended to put it to.

M'k'n'zy sat down, bracing his back against an outcropping of rock. He brought the hilt of the sword up to his teeth and bit down on it. And then he raised the welder to his face and flicked the switch. From the two prongs which extended from the top, a small, intense beam of light flickered for a moment and then held steady. He adjusted the controls, trying to bring it down to its lowest intensity, but even that looked daunting. He could not allow himself hesitation, however, for he felt blood starting to flow anew from the wound. He had no idea how much blood he had already lost, but if he didn't do something soon, there was no question in his mind that he was going to bleed to death.

The one comfort he took was that his face was already feeling so numb, he doubted he had much sensitivity left in it.

He brought the welder up to his face and took several deep breaths, once again doing everything he could to push away whatever pain he might feel. Then he touched the laser welder to his skin at his temple, at the top of the gash.

He immediately discovered that he was still more

than capable of feeling pain. A sharp hiss of air exploded from between his teeth even as he fought to keep his hands steady, struggled to make sure that his head didn't move. He bit down even more tightly on the hilt. He smelled meat burning and realized that it was him. He kept telling himself, *Detach. Detach. Ignore it. The pain is happening to someone else very far away. It's not happening to you. Watch it from a great distance and do not let it bother you.* And as he kept repeating this, slowly he drew the laser welder down the side of his face. It was delicate work, because—working entirely by touch—he had to hold the pieces of his traumatized face together and heat-seal them, while at the same time keeping his fingers out of the way of the laser itself. Once he got too close and nearly bisected his thumb.

He had no idea how long it took him to complete the grisly task. When he finished, the laser welder dropped from his numbed fingers. He slumped over, the world spinning around him, and it was only at that point that he realized he was still chomping down on the hilt. He opened his mouth slightly and the short sword clattered to the ground. He noted, with grim amusement, that he had bitten into the hilt so hard that he'd left tooth marks.

He was still chuckling over that when he passed out.

When he awoke, his first thought was that he had been lying there for about a week. He couldn't even feel his mouth; his lips had completely swollen up and gone totally numb. Blissfully, night had fallen.

The cool air wafted across him, gentle as a lover's embrace.

His mind informed him that this was the time to move. This was the time to haul himself to his feet and get the hell out of the Pit. It was always easier to travel at night. And he decided that that was exactly what he was going to do . . . as soon as he had rested up just a little more. He closed his eyes and—when he opened them once more—the sun was just starting to come up above the horizon.

And a creature was coming toward him.

It was small, scuttling, and seemed particularly interested in the pool of blood that had coagulated beneath his head. And, as a secondary curiosity, it also appeared to have taken a fancy to the newly soldered gash in his face. It had a hard shell, black pupils eyes, and small pincerlike claws that were clacking toward M'k'n'zy's eyes. Given another few seconds, it would easily have scooped out M'k'n'zy's right eye as if it were ice cream.

M'k'n'zy didn't even realize that he was still clutching the sword. All he knew was that, instinctively, his hand was in motion and he brought the gleaming blade swinging down and around, slicing the creature efficiently in two with such force that the two halves of the beast literally flew in opposite directions.

He smiled grimly to himself, or at least he thought he did, because he couldn't feel anything in his face.

Slowly he forced himself up to standing, his legs beginning to buckle under him before he managed to straighten them out. He tentatively rubbed the caked

blood out of his eye and was pleased to discover—
upon judcious blinking—that the eye was most
definitely in one piece. He surveyed his surroundings, confident in his ability to find his way around
in the Pit.

That self-possession lasted for as long as it took
him to get a look at his whereabouts. That was when
he came to the sudden, horrendous realization that
he had no clear idea where he was. "It can't be," he
muttered through his inflamed lips. "It can't be." He
had been certain that he knew every mile, every yard
of the area.

But he had collapsed right in place . . . hadn't he?
No. No, apparently not. Because now, as M'k'n'zy
ran the recent events through his head, there were
brief moments of lucidity interspersed with the
unconsciousness. He realized that, even barely conscious, he had started trying to head for home. It was
as if he'd been on autopilot. But because he'd been
operating in an ill, semidelusional state, he hadn't
gone in any useful direction. He supposed he should
count himself lucky; after all, he might have walked
off a cliff. Still, he had lost enough blood to float an
armada, he had a gapling wound on his face, he felt a
throbbing in his forehead, and his pulse was racing.
He had a suspicion that he was running a fever. Well,
that was perfect, just perfect. In addition to everything else he probably had a major infection of some
kind.

He looked at the position that the sun held in the
sky. Knowing beyond any question that he wanted
to head east, he set off determinedly in that direc-

tion. He didn't know, however, that he was concussed, confused, still in shock. Consequently, weary and bone-tired, he'd hauled himself east for nearly a day before he suddenly realized that he wanted, in fact, to head west.

By this time he couldn't move his arm at all, and he felt as if his face were on fire. But the sun had set, and he knew that there was no way he was going to survive another day of trekking through the heat. He could not, however, simply stay where he was, which meant that night travel was his only option. That suited him better, actually, because—despite his exhaustion—he was afraid to go to sleep for fear that he would not awaken. It was a concern that had some merit to it. And so, memorizing the point over the distant ridges where the sun had set, and using the stars as his guide, M'k'n'zy set off west.

He heard the howling of the storm mere moments before it hit, giving him no time at all to seek shelter, and the winds hammered him mercilessly. M'k'n'zy was sent hurtling across the ground like a rock skipping across the surface of a lake. And finally M'k'n'zy, who had endured so much in silence, actually let out a howl of fury. How much was he supposed to take? After everything that had been inflicted upon him by the Danteri, now the gods were out to get him, too? Couldn't he be the recipient of the smallest crumb of luck?

And the gods answered him. The answer, unfortunately, was to try and make clear to him that he was something of an ingrate. He was, after all, still alive. The gods, if gods there were, had permitted him to survive, and if that was not sufficient for him, well then here was a reminder of how grateful he should be. Whereupon the winds actually lifted M'k'n'zy off his feet. His hands clawed at air, which naturally didn't provide him with much support.

"Stoppppp!" he shouted, and then he did indeed stop . . . when the wind slammed him against a stone outcropping. And darkness drew M'k'n'zy in once more.

And the darkness tried to hold on to him as well, keeping him there as a permanent dweller. After what seemed an eternity, he fought his way back to wakefulness. By the time he awoke it was day again. His fever was blazing, his wound red and inflamed. He felt as if the only two things inside his skull were the constant pounding and a tongue that had swollen to three times its normal size. He now had a ghastly purpling bruise on the left side of his head to match the mangling of the right side of his face.

By this point he had no clear idea where he was supposed to go, in which direction lay safety, or even what safety was. His own identity was beginning to blur. He fought to remember his name, his home, his purpose. He was . . . he was M'k'n'zy of Calhoun . . . and he . . .

And then, like an insect wafted by a breeze, it would flitter away from him before he could quite wrap himself around it. He tried to chase it, as if he were capable of actually laying hands on a passing thought, and then he collapsed while at the top of a small hill. He tumbled forward, rolling down gravel which shredded his abused body even further. By the time he lay at the bottom of the hill, he was beyond caring.

He might have lain there for hours or days. He wasn't sure. He wasn't interested. All he wanted was for the pounding to go away, for the heat to leave him, for the pain to cease. How much was he supposed to endure, anyway? How much was he supposed to take?

He was tired. Tired of people depending upon him. Tired of people looking to him for decisions. All his life, as far back as he could remember, he had been fired with determination and singularity of vision. Obsession, some would likely have called it. Still others would have dubbed it insanity.

But behind the obsession or insanity or whatever label some would attach to it was his own, deep-rooted fear that he would be "found out." That deep down he was nothing more than a frightened young man, rising to the demands or expectations held by himself and others. As he lay there, feverish and dying, all the midnight fears visited themselves upon him, boldly displaying themselves in the heat of the midday sun. Fears of inadequacy, fears of not measuring up to the task he had set himself and the standard others now held for him.

It had been so easy at first. There had been no expectations. He had fired up his followers based solely on conviction and charisma. He had predicted success in battle, and then provided it. He had told his people that the Danteri would soon find themselves on the defensive, and he'd met that promise as well.

But as he'd taken the Xenexians step by difficult step closer to their goal, paradoxically that goal became more and more frightening even as it drew constantly closer. For two fears continued to burn within him. One was that, after all the effort and striving, the goal would be snatched from them at the last moment. And the second was that, if the goal was achieved . . . if the Xenexians won their freedom from the Danteri . . .

. . . then what?

He'd never thought beyond it. Indeed, the fact that he never had thought beyond it was enough to make him wonder whether he himself, secretly, deep down, didn't consider it a true possibility.

Get up.

His eyes flickered open, wondering at the voice within his head. It was the first thing he'd detected inside his skull in ages aside from the pounding.

His father was standing nearby, standing in profile. His back was raw with whip marks. The sun shone through his head, and a small creature scuttled uncaring through his foot. He didn't seem to notice. *Get up, damn you,* he said, his mouth not moving.

"Go away," said M'k'n'zy. "Go away. Just want to sleep."

Get up. I order you to . . .

"Save your orders!" snapped M'k'n'zy. At least, that's what it sounded like to him. Truth to tell, he was so dehydrated, his lips so swollen and cracked, his tongue such a useless slab of overcooked meat, that anyone else listening would have been able to discern nothing much beyond inarticulate grunts. "I begged you to stay! Begged you! Where were your orders, your pride, when I needed you, huh? Where? *Where?"*

Get up.

"Go to hell," he said, and rolled over, turning his back to his father.

There was a woman next to him. A naked woman, with thick blond hair and a mischievous grin on her face. She was running intangible fingers across his chest.

Get up, sleepyhead, she said. There was a playfulness in her voice, and something told him that it wasn't her usual tone. That it was something she reserved for him, and only for him. That in real life, she was tough, unyielding, uncompromising. Only with him would she let down her guard.

He blinked in confusion. He had never seen her before, and yet it was as if he knew her intimately. It was as if she filled a void that he didn't even know he had. "Who—?"

Get up, Mac, she admonished him. *We have things to do. . . .*

He stared at her. She had a beautiful body. A flat stomach, firm breasts. M'k'n'zy had never, in point of fact, seen a naked woman before. Oh, there had been women, yes. But it had always been rushed, even secretive, under cover of darkness or with most clothes still in place. He had never simply relaxed with a woman, though. Never lain naked next to one, never idly run his fingers over her form, tracing her curves. Never been at ease . . . with anyone. . . .

What are you thinking, Mac? she asked him.

He reached a tentative hand over to cup her breast, and his hand passed through and came up with sand. There was no sign of her.

With a howl of frustration (or, more realistically, a strangled grunt) he lunged for the place where she'd been, as if he hoped to find that she had sunk straight into the sand and was hiding just below the surface. Some sand got in his eye, and it felt like someone had jabbed pieces of glass into his face. He blinked the eye furiously until the obstruction was gone, but now his vision was clouded.

The world was spinning around him and this time he did nothing to fight it off. All he had to do was get some rest and he'd be okay. That was the one thing of which he was absolutely positive.

Yes . . . yes, just a little rest . . .

The ground seemed softer than he'd thought it would. Everything was relaxing around him, beckoning to him to relax, just . . . relax. That was all he had to do.

That's not an option.

It was a different voice this time, and it certainly wasn't female. He looked up in confusion.

There was a man standing there, shimmering as if from a far-off time and place. He wore some sort of uniform, black and red, with a gleaming metal badge on his chest. He was more or less bald, and his face was sharp and severe. Yet there was compassion there as well.

"Go away," whispered M'k'n'zy.

You're a Starfleet officer. No matter what you are

33

*now . . . that is what you will always be. You cannot
turn away from that.*

M'k'n'zy had absolutely no idea what was happening, and he certainly was clueless as to what this . . .
this transparent being was talking about. "What's . . .
what's Starfleet? What . . . who are you? What . . ."

You have a destiny. *Don't you dare let it slide away.
Now get up. Get up, if you're a man.*

There was a gurgle of anger deep within M'k'n'zy's
throat. He didn't know who this shade was, didn't
comprehend the things he said. But no one questioned M'k'n'zy's bravery. No one . . . not even hal-
lucinations.

M'k'n'zy hauled himself to his feet, adrenaline
firing him. He staggered forward, and the bald
taunter didn't disappear as the woman had. Instead
he seemed to float in front of M'k'n'zy, M'k'n'zy
steadily pursuing him. He continued to speak to
M'k'n'zy, but M'k'n'zy wasn't really paying attention to the details of his words. Indeed, they all
seemed to blend together.

And he heard ghosts of other voices as well,
although he didn't see the originators. Voices with
odd accents, saying strange names . . .

. . . and there was one word repeated. It seemed to
be addressed to him, which was why it caught his
attention. And the word was . . .

. . . *Captain.*

He tried rolling the unfamiliar word around in his
mouth, to say it. As before, nothing intelligible
emerged.

Time and distance seemed to melt away around him as he followed the floating, spectral figure. Every step brought newer, greater strength to his legs, and soon his pain was forgotten, his dizziness forgotten, everything forgotten except catching up with his vision.

It all came rushing back to him. The stories of the Allways, the visions of one's future that one could come upon in the Pit if one was open enough to them. The visions which had refused to come to him when he had sought them out. And now, when nothing concerned him—not even his own survival—that was when sights of the future presented themselves.

But was it the future? Or was it just . . . just fanciful notions from deep within his subconscious? That certainly seemed the more reasonable explanation. In his youth (odd that a man barely past nineteen summers would think in such terms) he had believed in fanciful mysticism. But he'd seen too much, stood over too many bloodied bodies. The fancies of his younger days were far behind.

But still . . . it had seemed real . . . so real . . .

And it was still there.

Still there.

That floating, bald-headed son of a bitch was *still* there, floating away, leading him on, ever on. M'k'n'zy let out a roar of frustration that, this time, actually sounded like something other than a grunt, and he ran. If he'd actually been paying attention to what he was doing, he would have realized the pure impossibility of it. He was suffering from exhaustion, blood loss, dehydration, and fever. There was no way that someone who was in that bad shape should be able to move at a dead run across the blazing surface of the Pit, yet that was precisely what M'k'n'zy was doing. And it was all happening because he refused to let that ghostly whatever-it-was taunt him this way.

"Who are you?!" he shouted. "Where are you from? Where's the girl? What's happening?! What's going to happen! Damn you, I am M'k'n'zy of Calhoun, and *you will not run from me!*"

There was a gap in the ground directly in his path. If he'd fallen into it, he could easily have broken his leg. It was five feet wide and eight feet deep. He leaped over it without slowing down in the slightest, and he wasn't even really aware that it was there.

And then he saw that the phantom, which was still some yards ahead, was beginning to shimmer. He got the sense that it was fading out on him altogether, and the knowledge infuriated him all the more. "Get back here!" he shouted. *"Get back here!"*

The specter faded altogether . . . but there was something standing in its place. Something of far greater substance, accompanied by a few other somethings.

M'k'n'zy's brother, D'ndai, stood there and waved his arms frantically. Around him were several other members of the search party, which had been wandering the Pit for some days in what had seemed increasingly futile search for M'k'n'zy.

D'ndai was a head taller than M'k'n'zy, and half

again as wide. He was also several years older. Yet from the way in which D'ndai treated his brother, one would have thought that D'ndai was the younger, for he seemed to regard M'k'n'zy with a sort of wonder. In many ways, truthfully, he was in awe of D'ndai. M'k'n'zy had always taken great pride in the fact that D'ndai was such a confident, trusting soul that he didn't feel the least bit threatened by the fact that his younger brother's star shone far more brightly than his own.

The relief which flooded over and through D'ndai was visible for all to see. He choked back a sob of joy and threw wide his arms, shouting his brother's name.

M'k'n'zy ran up to him . . .

. . . and pushed past him.

"Get back here!" he shouted at thin air.

The rescue party members looked at each other in confusion. On the one hand M'k'n'zy looked to be in absolutely hideous shape; on the other hand, he certainly seemed peppy enough for a man who was at death's door.

"M'k'n'zy?" called D'ndai in confusion.

M'k'n'zy didn't appear to hear him, or if he did, he simply ignored him. Instead he kept on running, gesticulating furiously, howling, "You don't get away that easily!" By the time the rescuers had recovered their wits, he was already fifty paces beyond them and moving fast.

They set out after him at a full run, and it was everything they could do to catch up with him. D'ndai reached him first, and grabbed him by the arm. "M'k'n'zy!" he shouted, keeping him in place. He gasped as he saw the huge gash in his brother's face close up for the first time. He tried not to let his shock sound in his voice. "M'k'n'zy, it's me!"

"Let me go!" he shouted, yanking furiously at D'ndai's arm. "Let me go! I have to catch him!"

"There's nothing there! You're hallucinating!"

"He's getting away! *He's getting away!*"

D'ndai swung him around and fairly shouted in his face, "M'k'n'zy, get hold of yourself! There's *nothing there!*"

M'k'n'zy again tried to pull clear, but when he turned to attempt further pursuit of whatever it was that existed in his delusional state, he seemed to sag in dismay. "He's gone! He got away!" He turned back, hauled off and slugged D'ndai with a blow that—had he been at full strength—would damn near have taken D'ndai's head off. As it was, it only rocked him slightly back on his feet. "He got away and it's all your fault!"

"Fine, it's my fault," D'ndai said.

M'k'n'zy looked at him with great disdain and said, "And what are you going to do about it?"

"I'm going to take you home . . . help you . . . cure you . . ." He put his hand against M'k'n'zy's forehead. "Gods, you're burning up."

M'k'n'zy tried to make a response, but just then the exhaustion, the fever, everything caught up with him at the exact moment that the adrenaline wore off. He tried to say something, but wasn't able to get a coherent sentence out. Instead he took a step forward and then sagged into his older brother's arms. D'ndai lifted him as if he were weightless and said, "Let's get him out of here."

"Do you think he'll make it?" one of the others asked him.

"Of course he'll make it," said D'ndai flatly as he started walking at a brisk clip in the direction of their transport vehicles. "He's got too much to do to die."

III.

M'K'N'ZY HEARD THEM TALKING in quiet, hushed tones outside his room, and slowly he sat up in bed. He was pleased to see that, for the first time in days, all of the dizziness was gone. He didn't feel the slightest bit disoriented. The pounding had long faded. In short, he finally didn't feel as if his head were about to fall off at any given moment, a state of affairs that could only be considered an improvement.

D'ndai had been cautioning him to stay put, to take it easy, to rest up. He was being extremely solicitous of his younger brother's health, and it was starting to get on M'k'n'zy's nerves. His impulse was to get out of bed and back on his feet, but D'ndai was always cautioning him not to rush things. It was advice that M'k'n'zy was having a hard time taking. It didn't help that it was, in fact, very solid advice indeed. Particularly considering the fact that the first time M'k'n'zy had defiantly sprung from his bed, proclaiming that he was fit and ready to go, the room promptly tilted at forty-five degrees and sent him tumbling to the ground. That had been over a week ago.

Now, though, the room graciously stayed put. M'k'n'zy padded over to a closet, pulled out fresh clothes, and dressed quickly. He didn't feel the slightest twinge of pain or dizziness as he did so, and considered himself on that basis fully recovered.

He stepped out into the hallway and startled D'ndai and the three other Xenexians who were holding a whispered conference. "Oh! You're up!" said D'ndai.

"How could I be anything but, considering the yammering going on out here," M'k'n'zy replied good-naturedly. "What's going on? What are you whispering about?"

D'ndai and the others looked at each other momentarily, and then D'ndai turned to M'k'n'zy and said, "Danteri representatives are here."

"Excellent," said M'k'n'zy. "You hold them down, I'll hack their heads off."

"They're here under flag of truce, M'k'n'zy."

M'k'n'zy gave him an incredulous look. "And you *accepted* it? Gods, D'ndai, why? They'll think we're soft!"

"M'k'n'zy . . ."

"If we showed up at their back door under a flag of truce, they'd invite us in, pull up a chair, and then

41

execute us before we could say a word. I say we do them the same courtesy."

"M'k'n'zy, they have Federation people with them."

M'k'n'zy leaned against the door, weighing that piece of news. "The Federation?" he said. *"The* Federation?"

D'ndai nodded, knowing what was going through M'k'n'zy's mind.

Their father had told them tales of the Federation in their youth. Stories passed on to him from his father, and his father before him. An agglomeration of worlds, with great men and women spanning the galaxy in vast ships that traversed the starways as casually as mere Xenexians would cross a street. Explorers, adventurers, the like of which had never been seen on Xenex except fleetingly. Every so often there would be reports that one or two or three Federation people had shown up somewhere on Xenex . . . had looked around, spoken to someone about matters that seemed to be of no consequence, and then vanished again. It was almost as if the Federation was . . . studying them for some reason. Sometimes it was difficult to decide whether certain such reported encounters were genuine, or the product of fanciful minds.

But this . . . this was indisputable. And then a chilling thought struck M'k'n'zy. "They're here on the Dentari side? Here to aid them in suppressing us?" A frightening notion indeed, because the stories of the Federation's military prowess were many. They might very well have been based on conjecture and exaggeration, but if even a tenth of what they'd heard was accurate, they could be in extremely serious trouble.

D'ndai shook his head. "I don't think so, no. They claim they're here to try and smooth matters over."

"Well . . . let them try," said M'k'n'zy. "Shall we go speak to them?"

"Are you sure you're . . . ?"

M'k'n'zy didn't even let him get the question out, but instead said quickly, "Yes, I am fine, I assure you. Perfectly fine. Let's go."

They headed down the short hallway to the conference room. The structure in which they were was, of necessity, rather small. Building materials were at a premium, nor was there any desire to make such an important building too big and, hence, an easy target. M'k'n'zy confidently strode into the conference room . . .

. . . and he stopped dead.

He recognized two of the three individuals he found waiting for him in the conference room. One was a member of the royal house of Danteri; his name was Bragonier. And the other . . .

. . . the other was the bald man from the Pit.

M'k'n'zy couldn't believe it. He resisted the impulse to walk over and tap the man on the chest to see if he was, in fact, real. He looked straight at M'k'n'zy with that level, piercing gaze which M'k'n'zy had found so infuriating. Standing next to him was the only one in the group he didn't recognize. He had thin brown hair, a square-jawed face, and wore a similar uniform to the bald man.

Bragonier took them in with a baleful glare. When he spoke he did not address the Xenexians, but rather the men at his side. "Are the people of Xenex not exactly as I promised, Captain?"

That word . . . *captain.* It so caught M'k'n'zy's fancy that, for a moment, he blithely overlooked Bragonier's snide tone of voice. But only for a moment. "We may not have your polish and breeding, Danteri," said D'ndai with a mock bow, "but we also do not share your string of defeats. We accept the one as the price for the other." At that moment M'k'n'zy wished that he had the sword with him. The one he had taken off Falkar. The sight of that would have likely sent Bragonier into total apoplexy.

But he needn't have worried, for his brother's words were more than enough to rile Bragonier, who began to rise from his seat. But the bald man standing next to him had a hand resting on Bragonier's shoulder. It was a deceptively relaxed hold. For when Bragonier tried to stand, the bald man was able to keep him stationary with what appeared to be no effort at all. And Bragonier was powerfully built, which meant that the bald man was stronger than he looked. And he radiated confidence.

"I am Captain Jean-Luc Picard of the Federation starship *Stargazer,*" he said, and nodded in the direction of the man next to him. "This is Lieutenant Jack Crusher. We represent the United Federation of Planets . . . an alliance of starfaring worlds."

Crusher said, "We have been . . . surveying your world for some time, and have made tentative first contact in the past. We feel you are culturally prepared to understand and interact with the UFP and its representatives."

"In other words, we've risen up to your level," D'ndai said without a trace of irony.

Nonetheless the irony was there, and Picard stepped in. "No offense meant. The fact is . . . the Danteri have asked us to aid them in this . . . difficult situation."

"Aid how?" D'ndai asked.

"To be perfectly candid," the man identified as Crusher said, "the Danteri Empire represents a rather strategically situated group of worlds. The Federation has been in discussion with the Danteri about their possibly joining us."

"But the Danteri seemed skeptical that the Federation had anything to offer," Picard now said. "However, they felt themselves stymied by the recent upheavals on this world. And their innate pride hampered their ability to discuss peace settlements with you in any sort of workable fashion."

"We could have," Bragonier said with a flash of anger. "It's not simply pride. It is them! They're savages, Picard! Look at them!"

Picard regarded them a moment. His interest seemed most fixed on M'k'n'zy, and M'k'n'zy met his level gaze unwaveringly. "I've seen worse," Picard said after a moment. "And you would be . . . M'k'n'zy, I assume?" His pronunciation was hardly the best; he tripped over the gutturals in M'k'n'zy's name.

M'k'n'zy made no attempt to correct how his name was spoken. He merely nodded, his lips pressed tightly together. It was a surreal situation for him, to be standing and conversing with a being who, barely a week ago, had been little more than a figment of his imagination.

"Your reputation precedes you," Picard said. "The Danteri have little good to say about you. About any of you. But that is of no interest to me whatsoever." His voice was sharp and no-nonsense. "I do not care who began what. I am not interested in a list of grievances. One thing and one thing only concerns me, and that is bringing you all together so that you can reach an accord. An understanding. A compromise, if you will, so the bloodshed will end."

There was silence for a long moment, and then M'k'n'zy finally spoke his first words to the in-the-flesh incarnation of Jean-Luc Picard.

"Go to hell," he said.

Bragonier's face purpled when he heard that. Crusher blinked in surprise, for he was somewhat unaccustomed to anyone, from lowliest yeoman to highest-ranking admiral, addressing Captain Jean-Luc Picard in that manner.

Picard, for his part, did not seem disconcerted in the slightest. Instead he said nothing; merely raised an eyebrow and waited, knowing that M'k'n'zy wouldn't let it rest there. Knowing that M'k'n'zy would have more to say.

And he did. "I know their idea of compromise," he said flatly. "Promise us a limited presence on our world. Promise us a slow pull-out. Promise us that we'll have self-government within six months. Promise us riches and personal fortune. And then yank it back at your convenicnce. Well, damn your promises and damn your lies. We want one thing and one thing only: the Danteri off our world for good. No contact. No overseeing. Forget we exist."

"I would gladly do so," said Bragonier tersely.

"Ohhh no you wouldn't," said M'k'n'zy. He leaned forward on the table, resting his knuckles on it. He was very aware of Picard's watching him, appraising him. "I know your kind. You will never forget. And you will never rest until my brethren and I are eliminated, and my people are subjugated. Well, I am here to tell you that it will not happen. These are my people, and to concede to you, to compromise with you, will be a betrayal of their faith in us. We will give them Xenex for Xenexians. If that is what you have come to offer, then offer it. Anything less, and you can leave."

"I am Bragonier of the royal house," Bragonier informed him archly. "You cannot simply dismiss us as if—"

"Get out," M'k'n'zy replied, and he turned and walked out. From behind him, Bragonier blustered and shouted. But he did so to an empty room as the rest of the Xenexians followed M'k'n'zy out.

They walked out into the hallway and started down it. And then, from behind them, Picard's firm voice called out to them. They stopped and turned to face Picard. Although Picard addressed all of them, his focus was upon M'k'n'zy.

"That was foolish," said Picard. "And you do not strike me as someone who does foolish things."

"Look . . . Captain," M'k'n'zy replied, "you've

just gotten here. I know these people. They are arrogant and deceitful, and think us fools. If we immediately listen to what they have to say, we will have to tolerate more of their condescension. There can be no peace, no talks, no rational discourse, until they are willing to understand that we are not their subjects, their slaves, or their toys."

Picard's hawklike gaze narrowed. "We will return tomorrow," he said. "And I shall make certain that Bragonier is in a more . . . positive mood."

"Whatever," M'k'n'zy said, sounding indifferent.

Picard hesitated a moment, and then said, "M'k'n'zy . . . may we speak privately for a moment?"

M'k'n'zy glanced at the others. D'ndai shrugged. M'k'n'zy headed to his room, with Picard following him. They entered and M'k'n'zy turned quickly. He never let his guard down for a moment, a trait that Picard noticed and appreciated. Picard took a step closer and told him, "These people listen to you, M'k'n'zy. They obey you. The capacity for leadership is one of the greatest gifts in the universe. But it brings with it a heavy burden. Never forget that."

"I have not . . ."

"You are in danger of doing so," Picard told him. "I can tell. You're filled with rage over past grievances. It's understandable. But that rage can blind you to what's best for your people."

"My rage fuels me and helps me survive."

"Perhaps. But there's more to life than survival. You must believe that yourself; otherwise you'd never have come this far or accomplished all you have."

Slowly, M'k'n'zy nodded. "Nothing is more important than the good of my people. All that I do . . . I do for them."

Picard smiled. "Save that for them. That's the sentiment they want to hear. But you and I both know . . . you do it for you. No one else. You take charge, you lead, not because you want to . . . but because you have to. Because to do any less would be intolerable."

Remarkably, M'k'n'zy felt a bit sheepish. He looked down, his thick hair obscuring his face.

"You're an impressive young man, M'k'n'zy," Picard said. "Rarely have I seen so many people of power speak a name with such a combination of anger and envy. You've accomplished a great deal . . . and you are only . . . what? Twenty-two?"

"Nineteen summers."

Picard's composure was rock-steady, but he was unable to hide the astonishment in his eyes. "Nineteen?"

M'k'n'zy nodded.

"And your goals are entirely centered around overcoming the Danteri hold and freeing your people."

"Nothing else matters," M'k'n'zy said flatly.

"And after you've accomplished that?"

" 'After?' " He pondered that, then shrugged. " 'After' isn't important."

And in a slightly sad tone, Picard said, " 'And he

subdued countries of nations, and princes; and they became tributary to him. And after these things he fell down upon his bed, and knew that he should die.'" When M'k'n'zy looked at him in puzzlement, Picard said, "A problem faced by another talented young man, named Alexander. For people such as he . . . and you . . . and me . . . the prospect of no new worlds to conquer can end up being a devastating one. In other words . . . you should give serious thought to goals beyond the short term."

"Perhaps I shall continue to lead my people here."

"Perhaps," agreed Picard. "Will that satisfy you?"

"I . . ." It was the first time that M'k'n'zy actually sounded at all confused. "I don't know."

"Well . . . at the point which you do know . . . let me know."

He turned to go, but stopped a moment when M'k'n'zy demanded, "Why are you so interested in me?"

Now it was Picard who shrugged. "A hunch," he said. "Nothing more than that. But captains learn to play their hunches. It's how they become captains."

"I see. So . . . if I had a hunch . . . that you were important to my future . . . that in itself might be indicative of something significant."

"Possibly," said Picard.

M'k'n'zy seemed lost in thought, and Picard once again headed toward the door.

And then M'k'n'zy said, "Captain?"

"Yes?"

"You, uhm," and M'k'n'zy cleared his throat

slightly. "You wouldn't happen to have brought a naked blond woman with you . . . ?"

Picard stared at him uncomprehendingly. "I beg your pardon?"

Waving him off, M'k'n'zy said, "Never mind."

"If you don't mind my saying so, that was a rather curious question."

"Yes, well . . ." M'k'n'zy smiled slightly. "Call it a hunch, for what that's worth."

Picard considered that, and then said, "Well . . . I didn't say all hunches were good ones. A captain has to pick and choose."

"I'll remember that," said M'k'n'zy.

He watched Picard walk out and thought for a time about what had transpired . . . certain that something important had happened here this day, but not entirely sure what. Then he looked over at his bed, thought about what Picard had said about dying in it . . . and exited the room as quickly as possible.

TEN

YEARS

EARLIER . . .

SOLETA

I.

SHE RAN THE TRICORDER for what seemed the fiftieth time over the sample she had taken of the Thallonian soil. She was confused by the readings, and yet that confusion did not generate frustration, but rather excitement. She had not known what to expect when she had first arrived on Thallon to conduct her research . . . only that the rumors which had reached her ears had been most curious. Most curious indeed.

Anyone watching would have found themselves spellbound by her exotic looks. Her face was somewhat triangular in its general structure, and her eyes were deep set and a piercing blue. She had thick black hair which was pinned up with a pin that bore the symbol known as the IDIC. Her ears were long, tapered, and pointed.

She had chosen what seemed to her a fairly deserted area, far away from the capital city of Thal. Nonetheless, despite her distance, she could still see the imperial palace at the edge of the horizon line. It was dusk, and the purple haze of the Thallonian sky provided a colorful contrast to the gleaming amber of the palace's spires. One thing could definitely be said for the Thallonian ruling class, and that was that they had a thorough command of the word "ostentatious."

There was a fairly steady breeze blowing over the surface of her "dig." A small, all-purpose tent, which collapsed neatly into her pack when not in use, was set up nearby, its sides fluttering in the breeze. She did not intend to stay overly long on Thallon, for she knew that an extended stay would be exceedingly unwise. For that matter, even an abbreviated stay wasn't the single most bright thing she had ever done.

She couldn't resist, though. The things she'd heard about Thallon were so intriguing that she simply had to sneak onto the home world of the Thallonian Empire and see for herself. She had been most crafty in arriving there. Her one-person craft, equipped with state-of-the-art sensory deflectors, had enabled her to slip onto Thallon undetected. Now all she had to do was finish her work and get off before she was . . .

The ground was rumbling beneath her feet. Only for a moment did she think it was a quake. Then she realized the true source of the disruption: mounted riders, obviously astride beasts sufficiently heavy to set the ground trembling when they moved. And from the rapidly increasing intensity of the vibrations, it was painfully obvious to her that they were heading her way.

She had been so preoccupied with her studies that she hadn't noticed it earlier. This was disastrously sloppy on her part; with her accelerated hearing, she should have heard intruders long before she felt them. However, mentally chastising herself wasn't going to accomplish anything.

Her pack was usually quite organized, with pouches and containers carefully chosen for every single item she might be carrying with her. And if she'd had the time—any time at all—she would have maintained that organization. But she had no time at all, so she quickly gathered her materials together, stuffing everything into her pack with no heed or care. She could have left it all behind, but she had no desire to abandon the scientific data she had gathered. One had to prioritize, after all.

She slung the pack over her shoulders and bolted for her craft . . .

. . . and stopped.

The craft was gone.

Her eyes narrowed and then she saw the nose of the craft protruding just above the ground. The entire thing had descended into what appeared to be a sinkhole of some kind . . . a sinkhole large enough to swallow her entire vessel.

She stared at the sinkhole and said flatly, "That was *not* there before. If it had been there, I would have not landed my ship on it."

Suddenly she looked up as, just over the crest of a nearby rise, several riders appeared. They were five of them, astride great six-legged beasts with gleaming ebony skin. One of the riders, curiously, was a young girl, several years shy of adolescence. She kept near one of the adults, a man who . . .

Well, now, he was definitely an interesting-looking individual. He held the reins of his mount with one hand, as if imperiously certain that the creature would not dare to throw him. It was hard to get a reading for his height since he was riding; if she'd had to guess, she'd have pegged him at just over six feet. His skin was the typical dark red of the Thallonian upper caste, and his brow was slightly distended. His head was shaven, and he had small, spiral tattoos on his forehead. His jaw was outthrust, his eyes rather small. Indeed, she would have not been able to see his eyes at all, had he not been looking directly at her. He sported a thin beard which ran the length of his jawline, and came to a point that made him look slightly satanic.

The girl to his right had skin a slightly lighter shade of red. Her head was not shaved, and her hair grew thick and yellow. But she had a single tattoo on her forehead.

Neither of them spoke, however. Instead the lead rider, a massively built Thallonian astride a mount who looked as if his back would break, said imperiously, "I am Thallonian Chancellor Yoz, and you are under arrest." He had guards on either side of him who glowered at the woman as if annoyed that she was disrupting their day.

As if he hadn't spoken, the woman pointed at the area where her ship had vanished and said again, "That was *not* there before. That sinkhole. The topography simply cannot change that way, not so abruptly."

Yoz stared at her as if she'd lost her mind. "I said you are under arrest. Submit to my authority."

"I'm busy," she said brusquely, her immediate difficulty forgotten.

The imperious-looking man at the girl's side half-smiled at Chancellor Yoz. "You have her nicely intimidated, Lord Chancellor. She should be begging for mercy at any moment now."

"Worry not, Lord Cwan. She will not retain her insolence."

"I was not worried," said the one called Cwan. "Worst comes to worst, she can always replace you as Lord Chancellor."

Yoz did not appear amused by the observation. Angrily he demanded of the defiant female, "What is your name?"

"Soleta. Now please leave me to my work. This is a scientifically curious situation, and it takes precedence over the famed Thallonian inhospitableness." She began to unsling her pack so she could pull out her tricorder.

With annoyance, Chancellor Yoz urged his steed forward and it moved with confidence toward the woman who'd called herself Soleta. She glanced with impatience at him and said, "Go away."

"Now you listen here . . ." he began.

With an impatient blowing of air between her

teeth, Soleta reached over and clamped her left hand at the base of the mount's neck. The creature let out a brief shriek of surprise and then collapsed. It rolled over to the right, pinning Chancellor Yoz beneath it.

Surprisingly, Soleta heard a peel of laughter from the girl. It drew her attention just long enough for one of the guards to pull out a weapon and fire it, point blank, at Soleta. It knocked her off her feet with such force that she felt as if she'd been slammed with a sledgehammer in the chest. She hit the ground and was busy making mental assessments as to just what precisely the nature of the weapon was when she fell into unconsciousness. And the last thing she heard was the voice of Cwan saying, "You certainly showed her who was in charge, Chancellor. Perhaps she *should* replace you at that . . ."

II.

SOLETA STARED at the four walls of the dungeon around her and wondered just how much one was reasonably supposed to suffer in the pursuit of scientific knowledge. Unfortunately, the skeleton lying next to her didn't seem inclined to provide an answer.

She suspected the Thallonians left skeletons lying around their dungeons for dramatic effect. Perhaps even to intimidate prisoners. Certainly it didn't seem to serve any logical purpose.

The dungeon itself was hideously primitive-looking. The floor was strewn with straw, the walls made of rock. It was a contrast to the other parts of the palace, which had a far more contemporary look. Far in the distance, her sharp ears were able to take in the sounds of celebration. The Thallonian royal family was having one of their famous "do's."

"Pity I wasn't invited," she said dryly to no one in particular.

She pulled experimentally on the bonds that attached her wrists to the wall. They weren't anything as arcane as chain, which would have been consistent with the decor. Instead they seemed to be some sort of coated cable. They were, however, rather effective. They seemed solidly attached to the wall, without the slightest interest in being broken by her efforts. They were firmly attached to her wrists by means of thick wristlets. The key was securely in the possession of the guards outside. She was having trouble brushing her hair out of her face since her movement was impeded. Her IDIC pin was gone; she had no idea whether someone had stolen it or if it was just lost in the desert. She was saddened by the loss. The pin had no intrinsic value, but she had had it for quite some time and had become rather attached to it.

Her chest had stopped hurting a while back. She was reasonably sure that the weapon had been some sort of sonic disruptor device. Very primitive. Also very effective.

She heard footsteps approaching the door as she had many times in the two days since she'd been tossed in here. She wondered if, as had been the case those other times, they would just walk on past. But then they seemed to slow down and stop just outside the door. There was a noise, a sound of an electronic key at a lock, and then the door swung open.

Standing framed in the doorway was the guard who had tossed Soleta into the dungeon upon the instructions of no less prestigious an individual than the Chancellor of Thallon. Standing next to him was another individual whom Soleta could not quite make out. He was cloaked and robed, a hood pulled up over his head.

"You have company," said the guard. "You can rot together."

Soleta said nothing. Somehow it didn't seem the sort of comment that really required a reply.

The guard seemed to display a flicker of disappointment, as if hoping that she'd beg or plead or in some way try to convince him that she should be released. It was a bit of a pity; in times past, he'd been able to milk the desperation of some female prisoners for his own . . . advantage. Ah well. If she was made of sterner stuff than that, it was of no consequence to him. For that matter, it meant that if she eventually came around it would make her capitulation that much sweeter.

He guided the hooded and robed figure over to the opposite corner of the dungeon. "Sit," he snapped, his hand tapping the sonic disruptor which dangled prominently from his right hip. The newcomer obediently sat and the guard snapped cuffs identical to Soleta's into place around the newcomer's wrists. The guard stepped back, nodded approvingly, then turned to Soleta. "In case you're wondering, you had a trial today."

"Did I," Soleta said levelly. "I do not recall it."

"You didn't attend. Thallonian law feels that

matters proceed more smoothly if the accused is not present. Otherwise things are slowed down."

"Far be it from me to stand in the way of efficient Thallonian justice. I was found guilty, I assume."

"The charge was trespassing," the guard said reasonably, arms folded. "You're here. That makes it fairly indisputable. The penalty is death, of course."

"Of course. Is an appeal possible?"

"Naturally. Thallonian law may be strict, but we are not unreasonable barbarians. As a matter of fact, your appeals hearing is scheduled for tomorrow."

"Ah." Soleta nodded and, with a sanguine tone, said, "You will be certain to come by and tell me how I did."

He inclined his head slightly in a deferential manner and then walked out, the door slamming shut solidly behind him.

Soleta turned and stared at the figure in the shadows. "Who are you?"

The figure was silent for a moment. When he spoke, it was in a tone that was flat and level, and just a touch ironic. "A fellow guest. And you are the famed 'Soleta,' I assume."

She made no effort to hide her surprise. "How did you know?"

"Word of you has spread. Apparently you dispatched the high chancellor in a manner not keeping with his dignity. Si Cwan informed anyone who would listen. He was more than happy to—what is the expression—take Chancellor Yoz 'down a few pegs.'" He paused a moment. "May I ask why you are here?"

She sighed. "Scientific curiosity. In my wanderings, I'd heard some rather odd reports about the surface structure of Thallon. Some very unique geophysical, high-energy readings."

"Your 'wanderings,' did you say?"

"Yes."

From within the folds of his hood, he seemed to incline his head slightly. "You are a Vulcan. Vulcans do not generally 'wander' aimlessly. There is usually more direction and purpose in their lives."

She was silent for a moment. "I am not . . . entirely Vulcan. My mother was Vulcan . . . but my father, Romulan." She shrugged, a casually human gesture which was in contrast to her demeanor. "I'm not sure why I'm telling you. Perhaps because you are the last individual with whom I shall hold a relatively normal conversation. I have very little to hide."

"Indeed." He paused. "You are far from home, Soleta."

She raised an eyebrow and said—with as close to sadness as she ever got—"I have no home. Once, perhaps, Starfleet. But now . . ." She shrugged.

"Ah," said the newcomer.

"'Ah' what?"

"'Ah,' the guard is returning as I had surmised he would."

There was something about the voice of the man in the cell with her that she found almost spellbinding in its certainty. For Soleta had undergone a tremendous crisis of confidence, and a man who was so clear, so in control . . . she could not help but be fascinated by such a man. Sure enough, a moment later—just as he had said—the door opened and the guard entered quickly. He glanced at Soleta and the newcomer. Neither had budged, of course. Soleta was on her feet but still nowhere within range of the guard. And the newcomer was seated on the floor with such serenity that it appeared he was ready to stay there until the end of time. Quickly the guard looked around on the floor. As he did so, he was patting down the pockets in his uniform.

"Problem?" asked Soleta. Not that she cared.

"It's none of your concern," the guard said brusquely.

And the newcomer, from his position on the floor, inquired, "Would you be seeking this, by chance?"

The guard glanced over and his jaw dropped. For the prisoner was holding up the electronic key. The multipurpose device that opened the door of the cell . . .

. . . and also the prisoners' shackles.

Barely did the guard have the time to register this fact when the stranger was on his feet. It did not seem possible that anyone could move so quickly. A second, two at the most, had passed in between the time when the guard realized his peril and when the newcomer was actually making his move. Soleta hadn't even blinked. It seemed to her that the newcomer had not even really moved with any apparent haste. It was simply that one moment he was upon the floor, and the next moment he was upon the guard. His hand snaked out, lightning fast, and for a moment Soleta thought that the newcomer was in the process of strangling the guard. Had he done so, Soleta would not have mourned the guard's loss in the slightest. Oh, she couldn't have done the deed herself, but she wasn't going to shed a tear if someone else dispatched him on her behalf.

But the guard did not die. Instead his head snapped around in response to a hand clamping securely on his right shoulder. Reflexively his hands came up, grabbing the hand at the wrist, but by the time his hands clamped onto the arm of his assailant, it was already too late. His eyes rolled up and, without a sound, he slumped to the floor.

"That was a nerve pinch," said Soleta.

The newcomer made no immediate reply, but instead took the electronic key, which he clasped securely in his palm, crossed quickly to Soleta, and opened the shackles that held her. She rubbed her wrist. "Who *are* you?" she demanded.

He pulled his hood back and Soleta found herself staring into the eyes of an individual who looked as if he could have passed for a Thallonian. His skin had the dark, almost reddish tint and arched eyebrows that were distinctive to Thallonians. His hair was long on the sides, and she looked inquisitively at it. In silent response, he pulled back the hair just a shade to reveal distinctive pointed ears. Vulcan. An older Vulcan, to be sure. He had the face of one who had seen every reason in the galaxy to give up on logic and surrender oneself to disorder . . . and yet had refused to do so.

"The skin tone . . ." she said.

"Simple camouflage, to blend in with Thallonians," he said. "However . . . your predicament put me in something of an ethical bind. I could have remained an impostor . . . blending in with the Thallonian people . . . but that would have required my allowing your demise. The security into the dungeon is too effective. Revealing that I myself was likewise a trespasser onto Thallon was the only means I could discern to get sufficiently near you to be of assistance."

"What is your name?"

"I am Spock," he said.

She looked at him, and her inability to disguise her amazement a sure tip-off to her mixed lineage. A purebred Vulcan would have made do with a quizzically raised eyebrow. "Not . . . *the* Spock. Captain Kirk's Spock?"

And now he did, in fact, lift an eyebrow, in a manner evoking both curiosity and amusement. "I was unaware I was considered his property."

"Sorry. I'm . . . sorry."

"Your apology, though no doubt sincere, is both unnecessary and of no interest." He glanced briskly around. "There is no logical reason for us to remain. I suggest we do not."

She nodded in brisk agreement. "You lead the way."

"Of course."

They headed quickly out of the cell, pausing only to securely close the door behind them. The guard lay on the floor, insensate.

They made their way carefully down a hallway. In the far distance they could still hear the sounds of merriment. The party was apparently in full swing. With no one around, Soleta could indulge herself in a low whisper. "I studied so many of your exploits, back in the Academy. It . . . it's difficult to believe that everything they told us really happened."

He paused, his back against the wall of the corridor. "Do not believe it," he said.

"So you're saying it didn't happen."

"No. It happened. But if it simplifies your life to disbelieve it, then do so. It is of no consequence to me. Of far greater concern is our departure." He started moving again, and gestured for her to follow.

"You said security was tight."

"Coming in, yes. Departing, on the other hand, may prove a simpler matter."

Indeed, Spock's theory was correct. There were guard stations placed at intervals along the way, but the guards were lax. Never within recent memory had there been any sort of breakout from the dungeon area, so no one anticipated any now. To exacerbate matters, the sounds of the not-too-far-off party were a sort of aural intoxication. The guards could hear the sounds of laughter and merriment and—most distracting of all—peals of feminine laughter. It was, to say the least, distracting.

Cataclysmically distracting, as it turned out, for Spock and Soleta had no trouble sneaking up on the guards and dispatching them from behind. Indeed, Spock found himself in silent admiration of Soleta's technique. She moved so quietly that it almost seemed as if her feet did not touch the floor. Her technique with the nerve pinch was not as sure and smooth as his, however. Spock had so fine-tuned his ability that the merest brushing of his fingers in the appropriate area was enough to dispatch his victims. Soleta, on the other hand, would grab her target with an almost feral ferocity. If there was a more deft means of taking down an individual by means of nerve pinch, Soleta didn't seem interested in learning it. She noticed Spock watching her at one point.

"Problem?" she asked.

"Increase the spread of your middle fingers by point zero five centimeters," he said. "You will find that you will render a subject unconscious precisely eight-tenths of a second more rapidly."

They came around a corner and suddenly found themselves face-to-face with a guard. He opened his mouth to let out a shout of alarm. Soleta's right arm swung around so fast that it seemed nothing more than a blur. It cracked solidly across the guard's jaw, breaking it with a loud snap that ricocheted up and down the hallway. He dropped insensate to the floor, unconscious before he reached it.

"Of course," Spock continued as if there had been no interruption, "there is something to be said for brute force."

"Thanks," she said. She had already unloaded a disruptor from the belt of one of the guards. She pulled this guard's disruptor from his belt as well and extended it to Spock. He took it, glancing at it in a sort of abstract distaste . . . as if he saw little use for it, but nonetheless had no desire to simply toss it aside. He tucked it safely within the folds of his cloak. "Why are you here?" she asked, taking the brief lull to inquire. "You're an ambassador now, but the Federation doesn't have diplomatic ties with Thallon. No one does. So why are you here?"

"As of late, I have been making inroads into such situations as these precisely because there are no diplomatic ties," he said. "Absence of presence does not require absence of interest. The Federation considers the Thallonian Empire of . . . interest. There has been much rumor and innuendo. It was felt that someone capable of passing as a Thallonian would be of use in investigating the territory."

"So you're a spy," Soleta said.

"Not at all. I am merely an operative for an outside government, who adopted an undercover persona and entered restricted territory through subterfuge for the purpose of discreetly gathering information that might be of use to my superiors."

"So you're a spy," Soleta repeated.

He gazed at her levelly. "Were I a spy," he advised her in an even tone, "you would still be in your cell, as I would be most unlikely to jeopardize my mission simply for the purpose of rescuing a single unrelated female whose own sloppiness placed her in harm's way."

"All right," she sighed. "Point taken. So . . . how do we get off of Thallon?"

"I have arranged transportation."

"What kind?"

"Swift."

She quickly realized he had no intention of going

into detail. In the unfortunate happenstance that she should be recaptured, he had no desire to risk her being forced to tell her captors information that could prevent them from getting offworld . . . provided, of course, that she were still capable of getting offworld. She nodded, acknowledging the brevity of the answer but not pursuing it.

As they got farther and farther away from the dungeon, Soleta was struck once more by the opulence of their surroundings. The royal family of Thallon was collectively every inch the image of the ruling upper class. There were tapestries hanging on walls, ancient pottery inset into the wall, assorted chairs lining the walls apparently for the convenience of any exhausted passerby who needed to take some pressure off his feet after an extended trek through the castle.

The sounds of the party were deafening, and Soleta momentarily wondered if Spock had lost his mind. Did he intend to audaciously walk into the middle of the celebrations? There was a boldness to such a plan that was almost attractive. It would mean that he intended to hide in plain sight. A cunning strategy that, indeed, might work.

But most likely wouldn't.

And it quickly became apparent that it was not his intention at all. There was a cross-corridor, and Spock gestured for her to follow him down. She kept pace with him, following quickly behind.

And then from around the corner stepped Si Cwan.

Spock and Soleta stopped dead in their tracks. Si

Cwan did likewise. Cwan was dressed differently than he had been before. In the desert he'd been clad in riding leathers, but here he was sumptuously done up in thick, gorgeously patterned clothes. A long flowing cape hung down from his shoulders. There was also a disruptor dangling from his hip.

Soleta did not wait for him to draw it. Instead she had one of the stolen disruptors in her hand, and she was aiming it squarely at Si Cwan. "Do not move or I will shoot," she said briskly.

"Are you serious?" he asked with unfeigned amusement.

His tone of voice annoyed her, and it was all the excuse Soleta needed. She squeezed the trigger.

Nothing happened.

She glanced at the level indicator in confusion. It read that the weapon was fully charged.

As if reading her mind, he said calmly, "Genetically encoded to its user. Just in case a situation such as this should present itself."

Of course, Si Cwan's weapon would work just fine. And there was no question whatsoever that he could draw the weapon and fire it, and Spock and Soleta were too far away from him to do anything to stop him short of groveling. And neither of them were the groveling type.

He had them cold. They knew it, he knew it, and he knew they knew it.

Yet Spock sounded so calm that one would have thought it was he who had the upper hand. "There is nothing to be gained by our continued incarceration," he informed Si Cwan. "You would be well advised to release us immediately, so that we may take our leave."

"Indeed," asked Si Cwan. "I doubt the Chancellor would feel the same way."

Before Spock could reply, Soleta drew herself up to her full height (which was still a head shorter than Si Cwan). "I want you to know," Soleta said stridently, "that I believe your so-called civilized society to be anything but. Your xenophobia and controlling impulses are ultimately self-destructive."

"Soleta," Spock said warningly.

Unheedingly, she continued, "I believe that your society will crumble within the next twenty years. From my reading of the outlying worlds of your empire, it cannot possibly sustain itself. Do with us as you will. Sound the alarm or, if you will, shoot us down where we stand. But be aware that our downfall will be followed, sooner or later, by your own."

Si Cwan eyed her with unrestrained curiosity. She wasn't quite sure, but it appeared as if, for a moment, the edges of his mouth were starting to go upward. Then his hand went toward the disruptor, and Soleta and Spock steeled themselves. Spock caught her glance and, with an almost imperceptible movement of his head, indicated to her that she should break to the left upon Cwan's firing, while Spock angled to the right. Perhaps, in that way, they wouldn't both be hit and a rescue could still be salvaged.

And then Si Cwan's hand went past the weapon and thrust into his pocket. He pulled something out in his closed fist, and then he opened his hand. Soleta looked in surprise to see her IDIC pin in Cwan's hand.

"My sister removed this from you without my knowing," said Si Cwan. "I informed her that theft was inappropriate behavior for a princess, and was on my way to return it. Thank you for saving me the extra distance." And with a flick of his wrist he tossed the IDIC to her.

She caught it expertly and looked at it with clear surprise. "I had not anticipated getting this back."

"Life is not anticipation. Death is anticipation. Life is constant surprise."

Soleta considered the situation and then struck a defensive posture. Her arms were cocked, her legs poised and ready to lash out. Spock, standing to her side, looked at her with as close to confusion as he ever allowed himself to come. "What are you doing?"

"In the event he intends to attack us by hand . . ."

This actually prompted Si Cwan to laugh. "As sporting as that might be, it seems a bit unnecessary." Then he pointed off to his left. "Go."

Soleta tilted her head slightly. "What?"

"Go. Leave. The way is clear, I believe. Depart." He paused and said in barely restrained amusement, "Unless you would prefer that I attempt to stop you."

Spock immediately said, "That will not be necessary." He put a firm hand on Soleta's shoulder and guided her past Si Cwan, who stepped to the side, arms folded.

As they headed off down the hallway, he suddenly called to them, "Wait." They turned and Si Cwan removed his cloak and tossed it to Soleta. She caught it reflexively and looked at it in confusion, and then at him. He gestured for her to drape it up and over her head, sporting it as if it had a hood. "It will make your departure simpler," he said.

Soleta couldn't help herself. "Why?" she demanded. "Why are you helping us?"

He smiled. "A typical scientist. You can take nothing for granted; you have to have explanations for everything, even good fortune." He stroked his chin thoughtfully. "It will annoy the Chancellor. There. Hopefully that will suffice. Now go . . . before I change my mind."

They did not wait around to see if that possibility occurred. Within minutes they were outside the palace. A couple of passing guards made no effort to stop them. It was entirely possible that they simply did not realize that these were escaping prisoners. On the other hand, it was also remotely possible that Si Cwan had somehow cleared the way for them. Either way, it was not a turn of events that either Spock or Soleta was in the slightest inclined to challenge.

They moved at a miles-eating clip until the palace was safely distant, and then Spock slowed his gait a notch. Soleta followed suit. "That was unexpected," she said.

"When I was in Captain Kirk's 'possession,' the unexpected became somewhat routine."

She winced inwardly. "Sorry about that."

"Apologies arc . . ."

"Unnecessary and of no interest, right, I know," Soleta sighed. "How do we get off the planet?"

"I have made arrangements. A private vessel, primarily a freighter servicing the Thallonian Empire. Sufficiently resourceful to slip in and out past border patrols. The freighter captain will meet us shortly and escort us from the planet surface."

She turned to face him. "Ambassador Spock . . . thank you. I have no idea whether thanks fall into the same category as apologies, but . . ."

"You are . . ." He paused, dredged up the word. ". . . welcome."

III.

SI CWAN STOOD at the window of a high tower and watched them go. His eyesight was exceptionally sharp; even from this distance, he could see them leaving.

Soon, quite soon, the fallen guards would likely be discovered. Si Cwan had no sympathy for them; if they had gotten so sloppy that two departing prisoners were capable of dispatching them, then they certainly did not deserve to remain conscious. They probably didn't even deserve to retain their jobs. He would give serious thought to firing every single guard and replacing them.

On the other hand, although he hated to admit it, he felt some degree of indebtedness to his guards' inability to keep the prisoners locked away. After all, if they'd been successful, Si Cwan wouldn't have had the amusement of letting them go.

Why *had* he let them go? He wasn't entirely sure. Perhaps it was the reason he had stated, for he truly was not a great supporter of the Chancellor.

Or perhaps it was simply a matter of repayment for the laughter that Soleta had brought to Kally. When Soleta had knocked the Chancellor's mount unconscious, Kally had erupted in peals of laughter that were extremely rare for such a serious-minded young girl. Si Cwan didn't hear her laugh nearly often enough. Yes, perhaps that was the reason after all.

Still, there was one dark aspect to it all: the woman's prediction that their society would crumble in . . . what? Twenty years? He was not particularly sanguine about *that* little prediction. No, not at all.

But it was just speculation, surely. And not even tremendously likely speculation at that.

There was a stirring at his side and he looked down. "Little sister," he said. "What are you doing here?"

Kally pulled at his robe. "Everyone at the party is wondering where you are, Si Cwan."

He bowed deeply, almost bending in half. "Merely awaiting the honor of being escorted by you."

She took his arm and, as they headed down a corridor in the direction of the merrymaking, she asked, "Where is your cape?"

He smiled, pictured Soleta's face, and said, "I gave it . . . to a friend."

TWO
YEARS
EARLIER . . .

SELAR

SELAR BARELY REMEMBERED any of her trip from the *Enterprise* to Vulcan. Instead, all of her attention was focused inward: inward to the urges that were rampaging through her body, to the drives that were sending her home as fast as the transport was able to carry her.

She felt as if her brain were being divided, with one part of her observing the other part in a sort of distant fascination. The cool, calm, emotionless assessment that had enabled her to diagnose so many people with clinical efficiency, was now contemplating her own state of mind. *So this is what* Pon farr *is like,* the Vulcan doctor mused. *A most . . . interesting phenomenon. Accelerated heart rate, unsteady breathing, a curious pounding that seems to mask out all other sensory input. I find it impossible to dwell on any topic other than mating.*

She had known of the Vulcan mating drive, had even seen it in action. But Selar had always imagined that she herself would somehow be less impacted by the primal urge. Actually, that was a common belief (some would say failing) among many Vulcans. So proud, so confident were they in their discipline and logic that, despite their thorough knowledge of their own biology, they had a great deal of difficulty intellectually accepting the concept of *Pon farr*. The problem was that *Pon farr,* of course, was the antithesis of logical acceptance.

Even when the first stages of *Pon farr* were setting in, Selar had not recognized them for what they were. "Physician, heal thyself" was a perfectly fine axiom, but the truth was that a physician was oftentimes not in the best position to judge what was going on in his or her own body. Such was most definitely the case for Selar.

The timing was particularly bad. She had enjoyed her duties on the *Enterprise,* and had looked forward to the many challenges that her position on the medical staff had offered her. But her physiology would not be denied. What had been difficult was having to be less than truthful with Beverly Crusher. She had not lied outright; she had merely told Crusher that certain duties on Vulcan could not be ignored, and that she would have to take an extended leave of absence. Despite the fact that it was one doctor to another, Selar could not bring herself to discuss such personal matters with an offworlder. It simply was not done.

Of course, Crusher wasn't stupid. It was entirely possible that Beverly knew exactly what was up. But if that was the case, then she respected Selar's privacy sufficiently not to press her on the matter.

So the leave was not a problem, and obtaining transport to Vulcan likewise was not a problem.

The problem, unfortunately, was Voltak. Voltak, her husband, Voltak her mate. Voltak, of whom she had only the vaguest of memories.

Despite her drive, despite her desire, there was something that lay at the core of *Pon farr* which was very daunting to her, and that was basically fear. Never in her life had Dr. Selar felt so vulnerable. Actually, never in her life had she felt vulnerable at all. She had always been supremely gifted and capable. But now, with her inner core laid bare for what she felt was all the world to see, she was driven to mate with someone whom she barely knew. Oh, they had kept up a correspondence, as much as her schedule and his had permitted, for Voltak had his own life and ventures to pursue. Voltak was an archaeologist, forever off on one dig or another, frequently in places where any sort of communication was problematic at best.

It was an infantile, childish attitude for her to possess, but Selar nonetheless felt as if this was all profoundly unfair, somehow. She was a private person, as were most Vulcans. And now she was destined to have no privacy, no barrier, nothing to hide behind, to be fully and totally exposed to a male who was, to all intents and purposes, an acquaintance at best.

And so it frightened her. Fear was something that she could deal with fairly easily when she was in her normal state of mind. As she was, though, she was hardly equipped to handle even the most casual of emotions, much less gut-wrenching terror.

The next hours were a blur to her, a red haze. She was met at the port by Giniv, an old friend of hers who was serving as the equivalent of what would be considered the "maid of honor." She was escorted by Giniv to a great hall. As was the custom, her parents were not there. It was not felt appropriate for parents to see their children during the time when such raw, naked sexuality ran rampant through them.

She sensed him before she actually saw him. She turned and saw Voltak enter from the back of the room.

Voltak was tall and strong, and although he was similarly in the grip of *Pon farr,* he was managing to maintain some degree of composure. Intensity radiated from him, drawing her like a beacon. Not only could she not resist, but she had no desire to do so. Instead her desire was for him, and only for him.

"Voltak," she said, her voice low and intense. "I am summoned. I am here."

She looked into his eyes and realized, to her amazement, that he had likewise been seized with similar doubts just before he'd set eyes on her. Oddly it had never occurred to her that the male would have anything approximating her concerns. But it was certainly not unreasonable. Voltak was no less proud, no less confident than Selar, and no less subject to the same apprehensions.

Those worries washed away from both of them when they looked into each other's eyes. They had been joined when they were mere children in a ceremony that neither of them could even really recall. But it all came rushing back to them, as the link which had been forged years ago finally took its full hold on them.

Selar loved him. Loved him, wanted him, needed him. Her life would not be complete without him. She had no idea whether the feelings were genuine, or whether they were a product of the heat of *Pon farr*. Ultimately, she did not care either way. All she wanted was Voltak's body against hers, to have the two of them join and mate, and fulfill the obligations that their race and biology put upon them.

The fear was forgotten. Only the need and hunger remained. Why? Because they were the only logical courses of action.

The Joining Place had been in Voltak's family for generations. Whenever one of Voltak's line took a mate, it was there that the Joining was consummated.

The room was ornate and sumptuously furnished, in stark contrast to the typically more spartan feel of most Vulcan domiciles. The lighting was low, the room temperature moderate. There was not the slightest discomforting element to distract them from each other . . . although, considering their mental and physical state of mind, nothing short of a full-scale phaser barrage could have pulled their attention from one another.

Voltak pulled Selar into the room and closed the heavy door. They stood apart from one another for a long moment, trying to focus on something other than the drive that had taken hold of them . . . although they could not, for the life of them, figure out why they should be interested in anything but that.

"We are not animals," Selar managed to say. "We are . . . intelligent, rational beings."

"Yes," Voltak agreed readily. He hesitated. "Your point being . . . ?"

"My point," and she tried to remember what it was. It took her a moment. "Yes. My point is that, rather than just giving in to rutting impulses, we should . . . should . . . talk first."

"Absolutely, yes . . . I have no problem with that." In point of fact, Voltak looked as if he were ready to paw the ground. But instead he drew himself up, pulled together his Vulcan calm and utterly self-possessed demeanor. "What shall we talk about?"

"We shall discuss matters that are of intellectual interest. And as we do that, we can . . . introduce ourselves to the physical aspect of our relationship . . . in a calm, mature manner."

"That sounds most reasonable, Selar."

They sat near each other on the bed, and Voltak

extended two fingers. Selar returned the gesture, her fingers against his.

It was such a simple thing, this touch. And yet it felt like a jolt of electricity had leaped between the two of them. Selar had trouble steadying her breath. This was insanity. She was a rational person, a serious and sober-minded person. It was utter lunacy that some primordial mating urge could strip from her everything that made her unique. It was . . . not logical.

"So . . . tell me, Selar," said Voltak, sounding no more steady than Selar. "Do you feel that your . . . medical skills have been sufficiently challenged in your position on the *Enterprise?* Or do you feel that you might have been of . . . greater service to the common good . . . if you had remained with pure research, as I understand you originally intended to do."

Selar nodded, trying to remember what the question had been. "I am . . . quite fulfilled, yes. I feel I made the . . . the right decision." Her fingers slowly moved away from his and reached up, tracing the strong curve of his chin. "And . . . you . . . you spoke once of teaching, but instead have remained with . . . with fieldwork."

He was caressing the arch of her ear, his voice rock steady . . . but not without effort. "To instruct others in the discipline of doing that which gives me the most satisfaction . . . did not appear the logical course." He paused, then said, "Selar?"

Her voice low and throaty, she said, "Yes?"

"I do not wish . . . to talk . . . anymore."

"That would be . . . acceptable to me."

Within moments—with the utmost efficiency and concern for order—they were naked with one another. He drew her to him, and his fingers touched her temples. She put her fingers to his temples as well, and their minds moved closer.

There was so much coldness in the day-to-day life of a Vulcan, so much remoteness. Yet the Vulcan mind-meld was the antithesis of the isolation provided by that prized Vulcan logic. It was as if nature and evolution had enhanced the Vulcan telepathic ability to compensate for the shields they erected around themselves. As distant as they held themselves from each other, the mind-meld enabled them to cut through defenses and drop shields more thoroughly than most other races. Thus were Vulcans a paradoxical combination of standoffish and yet intimate.

And never was that intimacy more thorough than in a couple about to mate.

They probed one another, drawn to each other's strengths and weaknesses. Voltak felt Selar's deep compassion, her care for all living beings masked behind a façade of Vulcan detachment, and brought it into his heart. Selar savored Voltak's thoroughness and dedication, his insight and fascination with the past and how it might bear on the future, and she took pride in him.

And then their minds went beyond the depth already provided by the meld, deeper and deeper, and even as their bodies came together their minds, their intellects were merged. In her mind's eye, Selar saw the two of them intertwined, impossible to discern where one left off and the other began. Her breath came in short gasps, her consciousness and control spinning away as she allowed the joy of union to overwhelm her completely . . . the joy and ecstasy and heat, the heat building in her loins, her chest . . .

. . . her chest . . .

. . . and the heat beginning to grip her, and suddenly there was something wrong, God, there was something terribly wrong . . .

. . . her chest was on fire. The euphoria, the glorious blood-frenzy of joining, were slipping away. Instead there was pain in her torso, a vise-grip on her bosom, and she couldn't breathe.

Selar's back arched in agony, and she gasped desperately for air, unable to pull any into her lungs, and her mind screamed at her, *You're having a heart attack!* And then she heard a howl of anguish that reverberated in her body and in her soul, and she realized what was happening. It wasn't her. It was Voltak. Voltak was having a massive coronary.

And Selar's mind was linked into his.

She had no command over her body, over her faculties. She tried to move, to struggle, to focus. She tried desperately to push Voltak out of her mind so she could do something other than writhe in pain. But Voltak, his emotions already laid bare and raw because of the Joining, was responding to this hideous turn of events in a most un-Vulcanlike manner. He was afraid. Terrified. And because of that, rather than breaking his telepathic bond with Selar, he held on to her all the more desperately. It is impossible to convince the drowning man that the only chance he has is to toss aside the life preserver.

Calm! her mind screamed at him, *calm!* But Voltak was unable to find the peaceful center within him, that intellectual height from which his logic and icy demeanor could project.

And in her mind's eye, she could see him. She could see him as if he were being surrounded by blackness, tendrils reaching out and pulling him down, far and away. Paralyzed, pain stabbing her through the chest, she didn't know whether to reach out to him as raw emotion dictated, or try to break off as logic commanded so that she might still have a chance of saving him. She elected the latter because it was the only sane thing to do, she might still have a prayer . . .

And as she started to pull away, Selar suddenly realized her error, because Voltak called to her in her mind, *My katra* . . .

His soul. His Vulcan soul, all that made him what he was, his spirit, his essence. Under ordinary circumstances a mind-meld would preserve his *katra* and bring it to a place of honor with his ancestors. But these circumstances were far from ordinary.

To accept the *katra* was to accept the death of the other, and Dr. Selar was not ready or willing to accept that Voltak was beyond hope, beyond saving.

She was a doctor, there were things she could do, if she could only battle past the accursed mental and physical paralysis that the mind-meld had trapped her in.

And in a fading voice she heard again, *katra*, and she knew that he was lost. That it was too late. Desperately Selar, who only instants earlier had been trying to pull free, reversed herself and plunged toward him. She could "see" his hand outstretched to her, and in the palm of his hand something small and glowing and precious, and she reached toward him, desperately, mental fingers outstretched, almost pulling it from his grasp, a mere second or two more to bring them sufficiently close together . . .

. . . and the blackness claimed him. Claimed him and claimed her as death closed around the two of them. Coldness cut through Selar, and for a moment the void opened to her, and she saw the other side and it was terrifying and barren to her. So much emptiness, so much desolation, so much nothingness. As life was the celebration of everything that was, there was death, the consecration of everything that wasn't. And from the darkness, something seemed to look back at her, and reject her, pushing her away, pushing Voltak and his soul forever out of her reach, for it was too late.

His *katra*, his essence, his life force, extinguished as easily as a candle snuffed out by a vagrant breeze, and Selar called out over and over again in lonely agony, called out into the blackness, raged at the void, felt his death, felt the passing of his life force, clutched frantically at it as if trying to ensnare passing wisps of smoke, and having about as much success.

No, please no, come back, **come back to me** . . .

But there was no one and nothing there to hear her.

And Selar felt a sudden jolt to her head even as the pain in her chest abruptly evaporated. Pulling her scattered senses together, she realized that she had fallen off the bed. She scrambled to her feet and there was Voltak, lying on the bed, eyes open, the nothingness of the void reflected in the soullessness of his eyes.

She quickly tried to minister to him, calling his name, trying to massage his heart, trying to *will* him back to life as if she could infuse some of her own life force into him.

And slowly . . .

. . . slowly . . .

. . . she stopped. She stopped as she realized that he was gone, and not all her efforts were going to bring him back.

She realized that her face was covered with tears. She wiped them away, composing her demeanor, pulling herself together, stitching herself back together using her training as a Vulcan and as a doctor as the thread. Her breathing returned to its normal rhythm, her pulse was restored to its natural beat, and she checked a chronometer to establish the time of death.

And Dr. Selar, as she calmly dressed, told herself that something valuable had been accomplished this day. Something far more valuable than just another mating for the purpose of propagating the race.

She had learned the true folly of allowing emotions to sweep one up, to carry one away. Oh, she had known it intellectually from studying the history of her race. But she had experienced it firsthand now, and she was the better for it. She had left herself vulnerable, allowed someone else into her psyche, into her soul. Certainly she had been dragged there by the demands of *Pon farr,* but she was over that now. The demands of her "rutting instinct" had cost a man—a man whom she had perhaps "loved"—not only his life, but his soul.

She would never, under any circumstance, allow herself to be ruled either by arbitrary physical demands, or by anything approaching any aspect of emotionality. She would be the perfect Vulcan, the perfect doctor. That, and only that, would be her new life's goal. For, to Selar, states of mind such as love, tenderness, or vulnerability were more than just an embarrassment or an inconvenience. They were tantamount to death sentences. And the premier credo of medicine was that, first and foremost, the physician shall do no harm.

That was something that Selar was all too prepared to live by.

Forever.

NOW . . .

I.

THE *U.S.S. ENTERPRISE* 1701-E made her way through space at considerably less than her normal, brisk clip. The reason was quickly apparent to any observer, for the *Enterprise* was surrounded by half a dozen far smaller, less speedy ships. Ships that had only the most minimal of warp capabilities, and at least one whose warp coils had overheated and was being towed along.

Looking at the monitor screen, in regards to their entourage, Commander William Riker commented, "I feel like a mother duck."

Data turned at this station and regarded Riker with such clear befuddlement that it was all Picard could do to keep a straight face. "Don't say it, Data," he pleaded, heading it off.

"'It,' Captain?"

"Yes. Don't begin inquiring as to whether Mr. Riker will begin quacking, or waddling, or laying eggs or acquiring webbing between his toes. The answer is no."

"Very well, sir," Data replied reasonably. "In any event, it will not be necessary, since you have already voiced all the possibilities that occurred to me."

Picard opened his mouth again, and then closed it. Riker and Counselor Deanna Troi exchanged broad grins.

"Although," Data added thoughtfully, "there is a *slight* tendency toward waddling. . . ."

Riker's face immediately darkened. The fact that Deanna was now grinning so widely that it looked as if her face was going to split in two didn't help matters. "*Mister* Data, I will have you know I do not, have never, and will never, 'waddle.'"

"You do tend to sway when you walk, sir," Data replied, undeterred and apparently oblivious of the imagery he was evoking. "A sort of rhythmic, side-to-side motion that could, under some conditions, be construed as—"

"*No, it couldn't,*" Riker said sharply.

"If you would like, I can demonstrate," Data began, half up out of his chair.

Both Riker and Picard quickly said, "*No!*" Surprised by the vehemence of the reaction, Data sat back down.

"That won't be necessary," Picard added, clearing his throat and trying to sound authoritative. "Data, I have observed Mr. Riker's . . . gait . . . on many an occasion, and I feel utterly confident in stating that the commander does not, in fact, waddle."

"Very well, sir," Data said.

"Good. I'm glad that's sett—"

"Actually, it is more of a swagger than a waddle."

Riker began to feel a distant thudding in his temples. "I do not waddle . . . and I do not swagger . . . I just . . . walk."

He looked to Deanna for solace and received absolutely none as she told him, "Well, actually, you do have a bit of a swagger."

"Et tu, Deanna?"

"There's nothing wrong with it. Actually, I've always considered it part of your charm. An outward display of confidence in yourself, your capabilities, and your position."

Riker drew himself up and said serenely, "Very well. I can live with that."

And then in a voice so low that only Riker could hear, Troi added, "Of course, that may in turn be covering up something . . . a basic lack of confidence, or perhaps insecurity with . . ."

He fired a glance at her, but before he could reply, Lieutenant Kristian Ayre at the conn glanced over his shoulder and said, "Sir, we are within range of Deep Space Five. Estimated time of arrival, twenty-two minutes."

Thank God, thought Picard. Out loud, he simply said, "Inform them that we are within range."

"There's a ton of ion activity in the area," Ayre commented after a moment more. "Thirty, maybe

101

forty ships have passed through here within the last twenty-four hours. They must be having a *lot* of visitors."

Riker glanced at Picard. "More refugees?"

"Without question," Picard affirmed. "Matters should be fairly . . . interesting . . . upon our arrival."

Picard had never seen a space station quite so packed. The place was bristling with ships, docked at every port. Many others were in a holding pattern. Some were in the process of switching places, taking turns so that different ships would be able to take advantage of the station facilities. The *Enterprise* dwarfed all the other vessels. Partly because of that, she wasn't even able to draw near, and settled for falling into orbit around the station, well within transporter range but far enough away that there was no possible danger of collision with a smaller ship.

At tactical, Lieutenant Paige said, "Sir, I have been endeavoring to hail DS5. There's a lot of subspace chatter, though. I'm having trouble punching through."

"With all the ships jamming the area, I can't say I'm surprised. The reports of the Thallonian refugee situation did not begin to approach just how comprehensive the current state of affairs is."

"Incoming signal, sir."

"On screen."

The screen rippled and the image of DS5 disappeared to be replaced by a face that Picard had not been expecting. Picard found himself staring into the stony, perpetually disapproving gaze of Admiral Edward Jellico. Picard could sense Riker stiffening nearby.

Jellico's history with the *Enterprise* was not exactly a happy one. He had never been a particular fan of Picard. Riker had voiced the opinion to Picard that it stemmed not from an assessment of Picard's performance as an officer, but from Jellico's likely jealousy of how well Picard was regarded by personnel both above and below him. Jellico had temporarily taken command of the *Enterprise* at one time, and he'd butted heads directly with Riker the entire time.

Jellico had a reputation for efficiency and for getting the job done, but he and Picard differed on a very core, fundamental issue. Men followed Jellico because, by the chain of command, they had to. They followed Picard because they wanted to, and no amount of blustering or authoritative officiousness on the part of Jellico was going to change that.

What it boiled down to was that Jellico's was a limited personality. He knew that he would go only so far and no further, would accomplish only so much and no more. Picard's vistas, on the other hand, seemed potentially limitless. Jellico would never be able to forgive him for that.

Perversely, Riker took a small measure of happiness in noticing that Jellico's already thinning blond hair was almost gone. Considering Picard's long-standing lack of follicles, Riker wondered why that nonetheless pleased him. He chalked it off to pettiness, but was willing to live with that. He glanced at Picard and saw no flicker of change in Picard's deadpan expression. Whatever was going through Picard's mind in relation to Jellico, clearly he had no intention of tipping it off to any observers. As always, Picard remained the consummate poker player. He got to his feet and faced Jellico, his hands draped behind his back.

"Admiral Jellico," Picard said evenly. "I was unaware that you were now in charge of Deep Space Five. Congratulations on your promotion and new assignment."

Jellico did not look the least bit amused, which was fairly standard for him. He never looked the least bit amused. "This is not a new post for me, *Captain,*" he said, emphasizing Picard's rank in a manner that did not indicate respect, but rather was clearly a not-so-subtle reminder of who was the captain and who was the admiral. "Although I've been cooling my heels here for so long that it's beginning to seem that way. Where the hell have you been? We've been here for three days waiting for you."

"We could have been here far more quickly, Admiral," Picard said, unflappable. "However, that would have required abandoning the vessels which we were requested to escort. Since we are supposed to be providing humanitarian aid, we could hardly do so by leaving behind those to whom the aid is to be provided."

Jellico gestured impatiently. "Fine. Whatever.

Ready the main meeting room, and prepare to beam us over."

"Here on the *Enterprise,* sir?" Picard asked.

"I thought my orders fairly clear."

"We had been told that the meeting would occur on Deep Space Five. . . ."

"I'm telling you differently. This place is a madhouse. Thallonian refugees everywhere, station facilities stretched to the limit. There are people camping out in the conference rooms, for God's sake."

Riker said in a low voice, "Ah, those irritating needy people."

He thought he'd said it quietly enough that Jellico didn't hear, but Jellico's gaze quickly shifted and homed in on Riker with daggerlike efficiency. Realizing that possible vituperation would hardly smooth matters over, Picard said, "There will not be a problem, Admiral. We can be ready for you by thirteen hundred hours, if that will be sufficient."

Jellico grimaced slightly, which was about as close to a nod of approval as he ever came. "Fine," he said, and blinked out.

"Perfect," said Riker. "Just who we needed to make a difficult situation just that more difficult."

Picard considered the matter for a moment, and then said, "I shall brief our guest on the change of plans." As he headed for the elevator, he called over his shoulder.

"Be of stout heart, Number One. We've handled the Borg. We can certainly handle Admiral Jellico." He walked out the door.

Riker turned to Troi and noted, "We aren't allowed to blow up Admiral Jellico."

"Regulations can be a nuisance," Troi said sympathetically. Then she seemed to brighten. "Don't worry. Perhaps he'll be sufficiently intimidated by your confident swagger."

Riker caught himself before he let his reply come out of his mouth, but he couldn't stop the thought. *Some of us have reason to be confident, Counselor. Others of us, who—for example—were unable to helm the* Enterprise *for more than two minutes without crashing her, have far less reason to be confident.*

As she sensed his feelings if not his words, Troi's mouth fell into a disapproving frown.

"I sense great sarcasm," she said.

Picard sounded the door chime, and a voice from within said, "Come." The door slid open and he entered the guest quarters. The room was mostly dark, with illumination being provided by a few choice sources of light including a lit mirror and a candle. To one side of the room, a man was seated in a most contemplative manner.

"Ambassador Spock," said Picard. "We have arrived."

Spock looked up at him, seeming to pull himself from his devotions with effort. He stared at Picard but said nothing.

"Admiral Jellico desired that the meeting be held on the *Enterprise,*" Picard continued. "Apparently there is an overabundance of activity on Deep Space Five."

"Indeed," Spock said after a moment. "The place is irrelevant."

Picard felt, ever so slightly, a chill in the base of his spine. Morbidly, he wondered . . . if the Borg ever assimilated the Vulcans, would anyone be able to tell?

"Will you require anything before the meeting?" Picard asked.

"No."

"Very well. I will have one of my officers bring you when the time has come."

Spock inclined his head slightly in acknowledgement.

No one had been more surprised than Picard when he had rendezvoused with the transport that had brought Spock to the *Enterprise*. Spock had been on assignment on Romulus. It was a measure of how seriously the Federation took the fall of the Thallonian Empire that they had requested Spock attend the Thallonian Summit. It had taken Spock no small effort to quietly extricate himself from Romulus. Still, Spock was one of the only people Picard knew of who had any familiarity at all with the Thallonians. It was only natural that his presence was desired at the summit.

He continued to gaze levelly at Picard. This was ridiculous. After everything that Picard had been through in his life, one would think that it would take a hell of a lot more than the stare of a Vulcan to leave him discomforted. Nonetheless, Picard felt as if he should say . . . *some*thing . . . but he had no idea what. "We certainly have our work cut out for us," he ventured.

Spock was silent a moment more, and then he said, "Captain . . ."

"Yes, Ambassador."

"Vulcans do not engage in small talk."

"Ah" was all Picard could think of to say. Then he nodded, turned, and started to walk out. And then, before he could exit the room, Spock stopped him with a word.

"Captain . . ."

Picard turned, waited with a raised eyebrow.

"I find," Spock said with introspection and not a little bemusement, "that I am experiencing a degree of . . . anticipation . . . in working with you again. The human phrase would be that I am 'looking forward to it.' " He paused, contemplating it. "Fascinating."

"The galaxy is infinitely fascinating, Ambassador," observed Picard.

"So it would appear."

"You know, Ambassador," Picard said after a moment, "Mr. Data—who was once even more removed from emotions than you—has recently acquired them. You might wish to take the opportunity to talk with him about his newly refined perceptions. You may find them . . . equally fascinating."

"I shall consider it, should the opportunity present itself."

"I'll see that it does. Oh, and Ambassador . . ."
He paused in the door.

"Yes?"

"This," and he waggled a finger between the two of them, "was small talk."

Then he grinned and walked out the door, leaving the ambassador alone in his darkness.

II.

RIKER REMEMBERED A TIME when he had gone mountain climbing at the age of fourteen, explicitly against his father's orders . . . or perhaps, if truth be known, precisely *because* his father had forbidden it. He'd been halfway up a particularly hazardous peak when his pitons had ripped loose from where they'd been wedged into the rock surface. Riker had swung outward, dangling, one thin rope preventing him from plunging to his death. The moments until his climbing partner had been able to reel Riker in and help him get re-anchored had been fraught with tension.

It was that exact sort of tension that Riker now felt when he walked into the main conference lounge. The sensation that a vast drop loomed beneath all of them, and they were all hanging by one single rope.

Picard was already there, talking with Ambassador Spock and a woman whom Riker immediately recognized as Admiral Alynna Nechayev. Nechayev was some piece of work. She and Picard had first butted heads back when the member of the Borg collective known as "Hugh" was aboard the *Enterprise*. Picard had refused to infest Hugh with a virus which would have effectively obliterated the Borg, and Nechayev had raked him over the coals about it. And they had had any number of fiery clashes since then. Yet now there she was, in the flesh, and she seemed to be perfectly happy to chat things up with the officer she had so mercilessly dressed down before.

Riker watched the dynamics of the Picard/Spock/Nechayev discussion, and it took him no time at all to discern what was really going on. He noticed that Spock was delivering most of his remarks or comments to Picard, treating him with respect and deference. It was only natural—or, if you will, logical—that Spock should do so. After all, Picard had put his own mind on the line to try and help Sarek, Spock's late father. Nechayev, by her rapt attention on the Vulcan, was clearly a major admirer of Spock's. That was understandable. The term "living legend" was overblown and pompous, but in the case of Ambassador Spock, it was also bang-on accurate. The fact that the living legend clearly regarded Picard so highly was obviously raising Picard in Nechayev's own estimation. She actually laughed in delight at some remark Picard made, and although it was obviously supposed to be something amusing, Picard nevertheless looked surprised at Nechayev's reaction.

Well, good. Picard had accomplished so much, and yet sometimes it seemed as if Starfleet regarded him with suspicion. Indeed, that they were suspicious *because* of everything Picard had accomplished. As if it were impossible to imagine that one mere mortal could have done so much. That it was . . . unnatural somehow.

In short, Picard could use all the support that he could get. If that support stemmed from Nechayev being a fan of Ambassador Spock, then fine.

That was when Riker noticed something out of the corner of his eye.

Riker couldn't believe he'd missed him before. There was a Thallonian standing over to one side in the conference room. He was tall, remarkably so. What was even more remarkable was that, even though the room was brightly lit, it seemed as if the Thallonian had managed to find darkness hiding in corners, behind chairs, under the table. Find that darkness and gather it around him, like a shroud, cloaking himself in the shadows as if he were part of them, and they part of him. For that matter, Riker wasn't sure even now whether he had spotted the Thallonian because he was sharp-eyed . . . or because the Thallonian had allowed Riker to see him.

He was tall and mustached, with spiral tattoos on his head. And he was completely immobile, not twitching so much as a muscle. If it weren't for the level, steady gaze he had fixed upon Riker, Riker might have wondered whether he was truly alive or a brilliantly carved statue.

Riker cleared his throat and approached the Thallonian. The Thallonian's gaze never shifted from him, and his face remained inscrutable. Riker came to within a couple of feet and stopped, as if the Thallonian had somehow drawn an invisible barrier around him and hung a large DO NOT CROSS sign on it. "Commander William T. Riker," he introduced himself. "First officer of the *Enterprise.*"

For the first time the Thallonian made a minimal movement: he inclined his head slightly. "Si Cwan," he said in a deep voice that was tinged with bitterness. "Former prince of the Thallonian Empire."

"My condolences on your tragic loss," Riker said.

Si Cwan gave him an appraising look. "How do you know," he asked, "whether the loss is tragic or not? If you believe the rhetoric of those who brought down my family . . . those who . . ." His voice showed the slightest hint of wavering before he brought it firmly back under control. ". . . who slaughtered those close to me . . . why, my loss of station is one of the greatest achievements in Thallonian history." He began to speak more loudly, deliberately capturing the attention of Spock, Picard, and Nechayev. "Our conquests, our good works, our achievements in art and literature . . . the fact that we sculpted order from chaos . . ."

"Gods spare us from more Thallonian rhetoric."

It was a gruff and harsh voice, and it came from the direction of the entrance to the conference room.

Riker saw Si Cwan stiffen as he turned to face the person who had spoken.

Standing at the door was Admiral Jellico. Next to him was Data, who had met Jellico at the transporter and escorted him to the conference room. Ordinarily protocol would have required that it be Picard or Riker, the ranking officers, who fulfilled that function. But considering the urgency of the situation, Picard felt it wiser to place himself where he would do the most good.

Next to Data was a squat and bulky young Danterian. His bronze skin glistened in the light. His broad smile displayed a row of perfect and slightly sharp teeth, and Riker found he had a barely controllable urge to knock one of those teeth right out of his head. The Danterian appeared insufferably smug as he studied Si Cwan, not even bothering to glance at Riker. The fact that he was being ignored didn't bother Riker one bit. He felt that if this Danterian looked at him for any length of time, he'd need a long shower just to make himself feel clean again.

Riker was not surprised by the presence of a representative from Danter. The Danteri were the Thallonians' "neighbors" over in Sector 221-H . . . a nearby, rival empire who were as ironfisted in their way as the Thallonians had been in theirs. But, the Danteri claimed, their ambitions were less overreaching than the Thallonians' and their own little empire more compassionate—a contention that did not hold up for anyone with a significant memory capable of recalling some of the fiascoes that occurred during the Danteri reign. (One of the best known was the uprising on Xenex, a rebellion that had lasted several years and wound up costing the Danteri a fortune in men, money, and esteem before they had finally washed their hands of Xenex and given the accursed planet and its inhabitants their freedom.)

"Thank you, Mr. Data, that will be all," Jellico said. His giving an order to one of Picard's officers in Picard's presence—particularly in a noncombat situation—was also a breach of protocol, and he fired a glance at Picard as if daring him to comment on it. Data, for his part, merely looked blandly at Picard. Clearly he wasn't going to budge until Picard had given his say-so. Picard caught Data's look and gave an almost imperceptible nod. Picking up on it, Data turned and walked out of the conference room.

"Admiral Nechayev, Captain Picard, Commander Riker, Ambassador Spock, Lord Si Cwan," Jellico said by way of brisk greeting. "I suggest we get down to business." He nodded toward the Danterian standing next to him. "This is—"

The Thallonian who had identified himself as Si Cwan stabbed a finger at the Danterian. "I know you," he said slowly, his already partly hidden eyes completely obscured by his dark scowl. "You are . . . Ryjaan?"

Ryjaan bowed stiffly from the waist. "I am honored that you know of me, Lord Cwan. One such as I knows of you, of course, but I am flattered that—"

"Save your flattery," Si Cwan said brusquely.

Ryjaan raised an eyebrow. "I was merely endeavoring to pay respects. . . ."

"Oh, Danter will pay," Si Cwan told him. "You and all your people will pay most dearly."

Picard stepped forward. "Gentlemen, little will be served by vague accusations of—"

"You are quite right, Captain." Si Cwan drew himself to his full height. Riker quickly realized that "looming" was Si Cwan's single greatest weapon. "So I will be blunt rather than vague. Our empire has fallen apart. Planets which once honored the ruling class have broken away. Our economy has crumbled, our social organization lies in ruins, and I have every reason to believe that the Danteri have a hand in it." He stabbed a finger at Ryjaan. "Do you deny it?"

"Absolutely," shot back Ryjaan heatedly. His cloak of deference was rapidly becoming tattered. "I completely, totally, and absolutely deny it."

"Of course you do," said Si Cwan. "I would have expected nothing less . . . from a liar such as yourself."

That was all Ryjaan needed. With a snarl of anger, he launched himself at Si Cwan, who met the charge with a sneer of confidence. Ryjaan slammed into him, and even as Riker moved to separate them he couldn't help but be impressed to notice that Si Cwan barely budged an inch. Considering Ryjaan's build and the speed with which he was moving, Riker would have thought that Ryjaan would have run right over Cwan. Instead Cwan met the charge and looked ready to lift Ryjaan clear off his feet.

"That's enough!" thundered Picard, coming from the other side.

Since Ryjaan was the aggressor, Riker and Picard focused their efforts on him. They pulled Ryjaan off Si Cwan as Admiral Nechayev stepped up to Si Cwan and said sharply, "That was completely uncalled for, Lord Cwan!"

"You do not have to be present at this meeting, Lord Cwan," Jellico put in. "We are extending a courtesy to you. Need I remind you that, officially, you have no standing. Deposed leaders do not rank particularly high in the grand scheme of things."

Ryjaan pulled himself together, steadying himself and nodding to Picard and Riker that he had regained his self-control. Picard glanced cautiously at Riker and they released Ryjaan, turning their attention to Si Cwan. Cwan studied them all as if they were insects.

And then, just for a moment, a cloud of pain passed over his face as he said softly, "'Uncalled for,' you say. Uncalled for." He seemed to roll the words around on his tongue. "Admiral . . . I saw good and loyal people slaughtered by insurgents. I saw family members carried away while I watched helplessly from hiding. *From hiding,*" he snarled with such self-revulsion that Riker repressed an inward shudder. "From *hiding,* as I foolishly let supporters convince me that it was important I survive. "For years my family knew what was best to guide the peoples of the Thallonian Empire. And someone goaded them, turned them against us."

"And you wish to blame it on us," said Ryjaan. "Go ahead, if it will please you, no matter how baseless the accusation."

For the first time, the ambassador spoke up. "The accusation," said Spock, "while inflammatory, is nonetheless logical."

"Logical?" Ryjaan practically spat out.

Spock was unperturbed by the vehemence of Ryjaan's reaction. "The Danteri share borders with the Thallonian Empire . . . or, to be more precise, the former Thallonian Empire. The Danterian desire for . . ." He briefly considered the word "conquest" and discarded it as too inflammatory. ". . . acquisitiveness . . . is well known. Overt action would possibly lead to undesired confrontation, and therefore it would be logical for the Danteri to pursue a course of gradually undercutting the structure of the Thallonian ruling class. Such actions would obtain the same goals as outright conquest without the proportionate risk."

Admiral Nechayev stood with her hands draped behind her back, and said with clear curiosity, "Ambassador . . . are you saying it is your belief that that was what occurred here?"

"I am speculating, Admiral," Spock replied evenly. "One could just as easily speculate that the Thallonian Empire collapsed entirely on its own, through a combination of mismanagement and oppression. The former would have assured the eventuality of disintegration, while the latter guaranteed that—when the fall of the empire did occur—the attitude of the oppressed people would be violent and merciless. I am merely playing devil's advocate."

Considering the slightly satanic look to the Vulcan

demeanor, Picard couldn't help but feel that some mild irony was attached to the comment. Seizing the momentary silence, Picard said, "At the very least, let us be seated and discuss the situation like civilized individuals."

"I heartily concur, Captain," Nechayev said. They moved quickly to seats around the large, polished conference table. The only one who seemed to be moving with slow deliberation was Si Cwan, who took a chair as far from Ryjaan as was possible. Nechayev turned to Jellico and said, "Admiral . . . it's your show. Walk us through."

"Thank you, Admiral." Jellico surveyed those gathered around the table. "Staying with what we know and what is beyond dispute: The Thallonian Empire has effectively collapsed. The royal family has been for the most part executed . . ." He paused to see if the harsh word had any effect on Si Cwan, but the Thallonian's expression was utterly deadpan. Jellico continued. ". . . as have local governors. Reports are muddled, however, as to any new government which may have taken the place of the royals."

"There is none." Si Cwan spoke up with authority. "I assure you of that."

"How do you know?" demanded Nechayev.

"There were factions," Si Cwan told her. "Many of them, united only in their hatred for the status quo. Hatred which had its origins . . ." He turned and fixed his gaze on Ryjaan, but then said simply, "God knows where. In any event . . . I know their type. The alliance will hold only as long as it took them to complete their bloody business. But when it comes time to work together, that will be beyond their abilities. They will tear each other to bits. The chaos and confusion which currently grips the Thallonian Empire is as nothing compared to what will ensue in the time to come."

"Lord Cwan's assessment would appear shared by the refugees," Picard now said. "For several weeks now, as you all know, refugees have been streaming out of the Thallonian Empire. At least half of them were sick, injured, barely alive, and many were dead or dying. The *Enterprise* was one of several ships assigned to escort them and lend humanitarian aid wherever we could. My ship's counselor, Deanna Troi, has been speaking extensively with some of the more . . . traumatized . . . individuals. They share stories of disarray, of internecine squabbling. It is not limited to the Thallonian homeworld, unfortunately. Various races, indeed entire worlds, whose antipathies had been held in check by Thallonian rule, are beginning to lapse into old and bitter disputes. Unfortunately our understanding of all that is occurring in the breakdown of the empire is limited by the fact that we know so little of the empire overall. Even the refugees themselves know or understand little beyond what was directly involved in their own day-to-day affairs."

"They had never needed to," Si Cwan said, and Riker actually detected a touch of genuine sadness in his voice. "We took care of them. We told them exactly what they needed to know, and no more. They were happy."

"They lived in ignorance," Ryjaan snapped back. "You did them no favor keeping them in that state."

"There . . . was . . . *order,*" Si Cwan told him, every word a bullet of ice. "That was what was needed. That was what we provided."

"Lord Cwan," Spock now said, "as you well know . . . I have been in Thallonian territory. I have been to your homeworld."

"Yes. I remember," Si Cwan said. Surprisingly, the edges of his mouth seemed to turn upward ever so slightly.

"My time there was far too brief to garner a full understanding of your empire's parameters, and the Thallonian desire for secrecy bordered on the xenophobic. It would be most helpful to these proceedings if you provided us with a more clear picture of what the Thallonian Empire consisted of. The number of systems, the more prominent races."

"The ambassador is correct," said Jellico.

"Of course I am," Spock informed Jellico, saying so with what sounded ever so slightly like amazement that Jellico would feel the need to point that out. As if Spock would ever be incorrect. Picard fought down a smile at Jellico's slightly flustered reaction, and in order to cover his amusement, the *Enterprise* captain said, "Such information would serve to guide us in our decisions. A course of action must be chosen . . ."

"Even if that course is to do nothing," Nechayev said.

"Nothing?" Both Si Cwan and Ryjaan had said the same word at the same time.

"That is certainly an option," Nechayev told them. "I must remind you gentlemen that we have the Prime Directive to consider. As disconcerting, as distressing as the current upheavals must be . . . it is not within our mandate to interfere."

"So you'll just stand around and watch all the star systems within the empire slide into oblivion," asked Si Cwan.

Ryjaan seemed no happier at the notion. "And you will let a member of the Federation—namely ourselves—deal alone with the security threat that the fallen Thallonian Empire represents?"

"You should have thought of that earlier," Si Cwan snapped at him.

Ryjaan was about to fire back a retort, but Jellico quickly cut him off. "We have not made any decision yet, gentlemen. As noted, that is the purpose of this meeting. Lord Cwan . . . will you tell us everything you know about the Thallonian Empire?"

Si Cwan looked slowly around the room. It seemed as if he were judging every single person in the room individually, trying to determine what he could expect from each and every one of them. Finally he said, "There were, at last count, thirty-seven systems within the empire. Each system has at least one inhabited planet; some as many as four."

"Would you be willing to work with Starfleet cartographers to give us a more detailed picture?" Jellico asked.

"Under certain conditions," Cwan said after another moment's thought.

"What sort of 'conditions'?" asked Nechayev.

"Let us save that discussion for another time. We must stay on topic."

"I'm curious, Lord Cwan," Picard said, stroking his chin thoughtfully. "What, precisely, do you feel is the 'topic' under discussion?"

Si Cwan spread his hands wide. "Is that not obvious?"

"Not necessarily," replied Picard.

"Gentlemen and lady," Si Cwan said, looking around the table and pointedly ignoring Ryjaan. "My escape from Thallonian space was aided by dedicated supporters, many of whom died in aiding me in my flight." Clearly the thought that he had, indeed, fled, was anathema to him, but he pressed on. "They felt that I was the last, best hope to restore the Thallonian Empire to its former greatness. And that I would do so by seeking your aid."

"If by 'your,' you are referring to the United Federation of Planets," Jellico noted, "need I point out that the Thallonian Empire is not a member of the Federation."

Si Cwan raised a scolding finger. "Do not confuse isolationism with ignorance. I point out to you that the Klingon Empire, some seventy years ago, also had not joined the Federation at the point that they found themselves in disarray. They were, in point of fact, mortal enemies. Yet the Federation welcomed them with open arms." His face darkened. "Perhaps we Thallonians should have sought conflict with you. Intruded into your territories, fought you for domination of worlds. Made ourselves a threat, rather than simply desire to be left alone. Had we done so, you might be as quick to cooperate with us as you were with the Klingons."

"Your description of the chain of events regarding the fall of the Klingon Empire," Ambassador Spock said with quiet authority, "is somewhat simplistic."

"How do you know?"

"I was there." He paused a moment. "Were you?"

Si Cwan met his gaze and then, to Picard's mild surprise, looked down at the tabletop. "No," he said softly. "I was not."

"For the sake of argument," Riker asked, "how would you have the Federation aid you?"

He looked at Riker as if the answer were self-evident. "Why, provide us with enough force of arms that the royal family can be restored to power. I know the power your fleet possesses. You have it within your power to right this great injustice."

The Starfleet officers looked at each other. Then Nechayev leaned forward and said, "Perhaps you didn't hear what I said earlier. Our Prime Directive forbids our interfering in other societies. . . ."

Si Cwan smacked an open hand on the table with such force that the table shook. "There is no society! There is disorder! Anarchy! I'm not asking you to change anything; merely restore the insanity which currently reigns into the order that previously existed. In exchange for your aid," he continued, "I guarantee you that the Thallonian Empire will be willing to join your Federation."

"It's . . . a bit more complicated than that,"

Nechayev told him. "There is an extensive approvals process through which any candidate must go. You don't simply snap your fingers and announce that you're in. Furthermore, you are not in a position to make any promises on behalf of the Thallonian Empire . . ."

"We were the Thallonian Empire, damn you!" Si Cwan shouted with such force that it shocked everyone into silence. For a long moment no one spoke, and then Si Cwan rubbed the bridge of his nose, looking a decade or so older than he had moments ago. "Pardon the outburst," he said softly. "I have not slept in some time. Being royalty does not make one immune from certain . . . pressures." He lowered his hand and then, with new urgency, he continued, "Let me put it to you this way: It is in the best interest of all concerned to restore the royal family to power. None of you knows what Sector 221-G used to be like. My kinsmen have ruled for two and a half centuries; an unbroken line of ancestors, keeping the peace, keeping order. There are some who might argue with the methods, but none can dispute the fact that for hundreds of your years, the Thallonian Empire thrived. I have many supporters still in place, but they are scattered and afraid. With the armed might of Starfleet behind us, however, it will rally support behind the true line of succession. Believe me, you would not want to see it return to the state that existed before my ancestors forged it into one of the mightiest empires in the history of our galaxy. If it *did* backslide in the anarchy that once existed, the number of dead and

dying to which you referred earlier, Captain, would be as nothing compared to what's to come."

And now Ryjaan's voice turned deadly. "That would not be advisable."

This tone did not sit well with the Starfleet officers. As much as he was trying to maintain his impartiality, Picard's tone was icy as he said, "Why not?"

"Because we Danteri have our own security to consider. In point of fact, we were intending to send our own vessels into Thallonian space . . ."

"I *knew* it," Si Cwan said angrily.

Ignoring Si Cwan's outburst, Ryjaan said, "To be completely blunt, several systems within Thallonian space have already contacted us. There is discussion of new alliances being formed. They want protection, and we are prepared to provide it for them. If a fleet of UFP ships enters Thallonian space with hostile intentions, it is entirely possible that they may find themselves in conflict with Danterian ships."

"You think to pick over our bones," Si Cwan said, and he started to rise from his chair. "You are premature, Danterian. We are not as dead as you would desire us to be. And if you come into conflict with us . . ."

"If by 'us' you mean your beloved royal family, need I remind you there is no 'us.' Your time is past, Cwan, and the sooner you come to terms with that, the sooner you can stop wasting our time."

"Sit down, Lord Cwan," Jellico said sharply, and

Si Cwan reined in his anger before it could overwhelm him. Slowly he sat once more.

Ambassador Spock, speaking in his slow, deliberate manner, said, "I believe we can all agree that avoiding violence and an exacerbation of an already difficult situation is of paramount importance?" There were nods from all around. "Very well. With that in mind . . . Ryjaan, you are authorized to speak on behalf of your government, I take it?"

"Of course. And you are for yours?"

Spock glanced at Jellico and Nechayev and said, "We have not come into this situation unprepared. I have made a thorough study and report of the likely reactions of both the Danteri and the Thallonians. Thus far they have remained in line with the projected probability curve."

Ryjaan made no effort to disguise his confusion upon hearing this pronouncement. Remarkably, he looked to Si Cwan for clarification. "He's saying we're predictable," Si Cwan explained.

"Quite so," affirmed Spock. "With that in mind . . . I have already made recommendations to the Federation which, if I am not mistaken, Admiral Nechayev is prepared to discuss."

"Thank you, Ambassador," she said. She drummed her fingers on the desk for a moment, gathering her thoughts. "Ryjaan . . . since the Danteri are members of the UFP, I am informing you that the Federation would consider it contrary to its best interests to have Danterian ships entering Thallonian space in any great numbers, inflaming an already inflammatory situation and stirring up hostilities. I am telling you this informally. If you desire, a formal resolution can be delivered by the Council."

"I see," said Ryjaan dryly. "And you anticipate that the Danteri will simply sit back and take no action, allowing the Federation to enter Thallonian space in force and shift the balance of power in a direction they find more appealing. Is that it?"

"No. That is not it at all. Provided that the Danteri do not, by force of arms, attempt to affect the situation, the Federation has no intention of attempting similar tactics, simply for," and she afforded Si Cwan a quick glance, "the personal benefit of a handful of people."

Si Cwan stiffened. "You do not understand," he said. "This has nothing to do with personal aggrandizement. I didn't ask for my station in life. To be relieved of responsibility . . . to be normal . . ." He took a deep sigh, and there was the slightest tremble to his words. "It would almost be a blessing." Then he seemed to shake it off and, more firmly, he continued, "It is not for myself that I seek your help. It is for the good of the entire Thallonian Empire."

"You," Ryjaan said coolly, "are not in a position to decide the welfare of the Thallonian Empire."

Before Si Cwan could shoot back a response, Jellico quickly stepped in. "It's irrelevant to discuss the option. Starfleet is not going to send in armed forces to restore you or any surviving members of the royal family to power, Lord Cwan. It simply isn't our way."

"I see. Instead your way is to allow billions of people to be swallowed by a spiral of chaos."

Spock replied, "That, sir, is overstated. It is also inaccurate."

"We are discussing," Jellico continued, "sending in observers. A neutral vessel with a small crew to observe and report back to the Federation, so that appropriate action can be taken at the appropriate time."

With utter contempt, Si Cwan said, "What a disappointment the present human race would be to its ancestors. As opposed to the pioneers and warriors of a bygone day, you are now all tentative and hesitant. When a time calls for the strides of a giant, you take small, mincing steps."

"Considering you came to us for help, Lord Cwan," Jellico said in exasperation, "I can't say I appreciate your attitude."

And then Commander Riker said something completely unexpected.

"Cwan is right."

If Riker had sprouted a third eye he could not have gotten any more of an astounded reaction from Jellico, Nechayev, and Ryjaan. Spock, as was his custom, remained impassive, and Picard was poker-faced.

"Are you saying we should go in there with guns blazing, Commander?" Nechayev said with ill-disguised incredulity.

"No," Riker replied flatly. "Difficult times do not call for extreme measures. But by the same token," and he leaned forward, arms on the table, fingers interlaced tightly, "we are talking about the collapse of an empire. We are, as Lord Cwan said, considering the fate of billions of people. For the Federation response to simply be that of passive observation . . ."

"The Prime Directive . . ." began Jellico.

"The Prime Directive, Admiral, last time I checked, did not first appear on the wall of Starfleet Headquarters in flaming letters accompanied by a sepulchral voice intoning, 'Thou Shalt Not Butt In,'" Riker said flatly. "It's a guide for day-to-day interaction with developing races so that we don't have umpty-ump Starfleet officers running around playing god by their own rules. But this is not day-to-day, Admiral. And we're not talking about playing god. We're talking about showing compassion for fellow living beings. Tell me, Admiral, while you were sitting on Deep Space Five waiting for us to show up, did you actually walk around and interact with the refugees? Did you see the misery in their faces, the fear in their eyes? Did you help patch up the wounded, stand by the bedside of the dying, say a prayer for the dead? Or did you sit isolated in your quarters grumbling over the inconvenience?"

"That is quite enough, Commander!" Admiral Nechayev said sharply.

Jellico smiled grimly. "You'll have to forgive the commander. He and I have some . . . history . . . together. The kind of history that prompts him to throw caution to the wind, even in the face of potentially gross insubordination."

If Riker seemed at all intimidated, he didn't show it. "The Prime Directive was created by men and women, no better or worse than any of us, and I respectfully submit that if our hands are so completely tied by it that we sit around impotently, then we have to seriously reconsider what the hell it is we're all about."

Jellico's anger seemed to be growing exponentially, but the supernaturally calm voice of Ambassador Spock cut in before Jellico could say anything. "I once knew a man," he said quietly, "who would have agreed with you." There was a pause as Spock's words sank in, and then he continued, "What would you suggest, Commander?"

"We assign a starship to enter Thallonian space. A single starship . . . hardly a fleet," he said, the latter comment directed at Ryjaan who already seemed to be bristling. "That ship will serve to report to the Federation about what they find within Thallonian space . . . but will also have the latitude to lend humanitarian aid where needed. Furthermore, if the races in question turn to the captain of this starship for aid in rebuilding their empire through whatever *peaceful* means are available," and when he emphasized the word he looked straight at Si Cwan, "the starship would basically do whatever is necessary— within reason—to try and make Sector 221-G a going concern again."

"And who decides what is 'within reason'?" demanded Jellico.

"The captain, of course."

"You want to send a starship into a potentially incendiary position, with possible enemies all around them, any of whom might want their help one moment and then turn on them the next." Jellico shook his head. "Putting aside the battering the fleet took in the last Borg engagement . . . forgetting for a moment that it would simply be sloppy planning to put a ship on such a detail for the benefit of a non-Federation member, and for an indefinite period of time . . . the bottom line is that Sector 221-G is a powder keg and Commander Riker is suggesting that we ask someone to stick their head into the lion's mouth."

"I would have phrased it without mixed metaphors, but yes, that's correct," said Riker.

Jellico looked unamused; it was an easy look for him. "It's sloppy thinking, Commander. It is a completely unnecessary risk."

And Ambassador Spock fixed Jellico with a dead-eyed stare and said, "Risk . . . Admiral . . . is our business."

Jellico opened his mouth, but there was something in Spock's gaze that caused him to snap it shut again. There was silence in the room for a long moment, and then Admiral Nechayev turned in her chair and said, "Captain Picard . . . what do you think?"

He tapped his fingertips on the table thoughtfully and then said, "I agree with Commander Riker."

"Oh, *there's* a surprise," snapped Jellico.

"With all due respect, Admiral, you know me well enough to know I would not speak from some sort of knee-jerk loyalty," Picard informed him archly. "I have respect for the chain of command, and for personal loyalty, but first and foremost I do what I feel to be right. Might I point out that if that were not the case, the *Enterprise* would never have joined the fleet in the recent Borg invasion and you would have far greater problems to deal with than what to do about Sector 221-G."

Jellico's face reddened slightly. Nechayev seemed unperturbed as she said, "Point well taken, Captain Picard. Admiral . . . I believe the idea has merit. It may take a bit of doing, but I'm reasonably certain I can sell the notion to the Federation."

"Admiral," began Jellico.

But Nechayev was making it quite clear that she was not looking for further discussion. "Do you have a recommendation for an available starship, Admiral?"

"I . . ." He started to protest again, but then he saw the look of steel in her eyes. He came to the realization that further dispute on his part was simply going to provide amusement for Picard and Riker, and he'd be damned if he gave them the satisfaction. So instead he switched mental tracks and began running through available ships in his mind. Finally he said, "One comes to mind. The *Excalibur.*"

"Wasn't she damaged in the recent Borg invasion?" asked Picard.

"Yes, and her captain killed. Korsmo. A good man."

"We came up through the Academy together," Picard said. "And I had the . . . honor of battling at his side in an earlier Borg incident. He was . . . a brave man."

"Yes, and his last act was to get his ship clear. Otherwise the damage could have been a lot worse. She's currently being refit and repaired. The crew has been reassigned . . . all except the first officer. She's awaiting a new assignment; she's angling for command."

"Aren't they all?" smiled Riker.

Jellico fixed him with a stare. "Not all," he said snidely. And Jellico took some small measure of satisfaction in watching Riker's face fall. "The *Excalibur* should be ready to go in approximately three weeks. Push comes to shove, we can probably have her ready in two."

"Very well," said Nechayev. "Admiral, Captain . . . under the circumstances, I would look to you for recommendations as to the appropriate captain for this assignment. We shall reconvene in your office, Picard, in two hours. Gentlemen," and she looked at Ryjaan and Si Cwan, "it is our hope that this decision will meet with your approval. It is, to my mind, the best we can offer at the present time."

"My government will be satisfied," Ryjaan said evenly.

All eyes turned to Si Cwan as he sat there for a moment, apparently contemplating empty air. When he spoke, it surprised all of them as he said, "I will, of course, be on this vessel as well."

The Starfleet personnel looked at each other in mild confusion. "Why do you make that assumption, Lord Cwan?" asked Nechayev.

"It is my right," he said. "It is my people, my territory. As you say, you thrust yourselves into a dangerous situation. I still have many supporters, and my presence will give validity to your own. I must be there."

"We protest!" shouted Ryjaan, thumping his fist on the table.

"Save the protest," Jellico said. "Lord Cwan, it's not possible. You're not Starfleet personnel."

"The idea has merit," Picard said slowly. "We are talking about an unexplored, unknown area of space. His presence could offer advantages . . ."

"I said no, Picard. What part of 'no' don't you get?"

"I'm simply saying you should not dismiss the idea out of hand. . . ."

"Look, Captain . . . perhaps some of us are so lax about the presence of non-Starfleet personnel that they'll let teenage boys on their bridge to steer the ship," Jellico snapped. "Others of us, however, know what is and what is not appropriate. Si Cwan has no business serving in any sort of official capacity on a starship, and I won't allow it."

Now it was Picard who was beginning to get angry at Jellico's digs, but Nechayev stepped in before the meeting could escalate in hostility. "Captain, I must agree with the Admiral. Lord Si Cwan . . . I must respectfully reject your request. I am sorry."

Si Cwan rose from his chair and loomed over them. "No," he said. "You are not sorry. But you will be."

He headed for the door and Nechayev called after him, "Is that a threat, Lord Cwan?"

He walked out without slowing as he called over his shoulder. "No. A prediction."

III.

"*Calhoun?!*"

In Picard's office, Jellico was making no attempt to hide his astonishment. He said again, "Calhoun? You don't mean Mackenzie Calhoun?"

"I most certainly do," said Picard, unflappably sipping his tea.

Jellico looked to Nechayev for some sort of confirmation that he was hearing a notion that was clearly insane. Nechayev was also surprised, but she hid it better. "I must admit, Captain, that I was under the impression you were going to recommend Riker for the position. That's the reason I didn't ask him to be here for this meeting."

"If Riker were interested, he would have let me know," Picard said reasonably. "Besides, I think

Calhoun would be far more appropriate for the assignment."

"Picard, in case you haven't noticed, the man *resigned*. Calhoun is no longer a member of Starfleet. He hasn't been for . . . what, five years? Six?"

"Officially, he took leave."

"Officially? The man told me to go to hell! He stormed out of my office! He's floated from one job to another, some of them exceedingly shady! Do those sound like the actions of a man who has any intention of, or interest in, coming back to Starfleet?"

" 'Shady?' " asked Picard.

"There have been rumors," Jellico said. "I've heard dabbling in slave trade . . . gun running . . ."

"That's absurd. We can't be guided by rumors and innuendo."

"True enough," Nechayev said, "but we must be cautious."

"Face it, Picard, he was a troublemaker even when he was in the Academy. The fact that he was your protégé . . ."

"He was *not* my 'protégé,' " Picard replied. "He was simply a damned fine officer. One of the best we ever turned out." He put down his cup and began to tick off reasons on his fingers. "He knows that region of space. His homeworld, Xenex, is right up against the Thallonian frontier, and he did some exploration of the territory after he left Xenex, but before he came to the Academy. Furthermore, he knows the Danteri, in case they are involved somehow with the fall of the Thallonian Empire . . . and, Ryjaan's indignation aside, I believe that may very well be the case. Above all, Admirals, let us not delude ourselves. If the Thallonian Empire is falling apart, you're talking about planets at war with each other. Angry factions at every turn. You need someone who can pull worlds together. Calhoun has done that. He was doing it when he was still in his late teens. We need that strength and skill now, more than ever before."

"He's unpredictable," Jellico said.

"So are the circumstances. They'll be well suited."

"He's a maverick. He's a troublemaker, he's—"

"Admiral," said Nechayev, "instead of complaining, may I ask whom you recommend?"

"The first officer of the *Excalibur*," Jellico replied promptly. "Commander Elizabeth Paula Shelby."

"Shelby?" said Picard.

"You are familiar with her, as I recall."

"Oh yes," Picard said with a thin smile. "It is probably fortunate that Commander Riker isn't here; he'd be chewing neutronium about now. They did not exactly hit it off when she served aboard the *Enterprise* . . . particularly when he was busy trying to clean her footprints off his back."

"Shelby is a solid, aggressive officer," continued Jellico. "She learned a good deal from Korsmo. She deserves her own command."

"She very likely does, but I do not feel that this is it," said Picard. "The unique situation, the challenges it presents . . . Calhoun is simply better suited."

"You're trying to put a cowboy in the captain's chair," Jellico told him.

"Absolutely," Picard replied. "This is a new frontier. Who better to send in to try and ride herd on it than a cowboy?"

"All right, gentlemen," said Nechayev. "I'd like formal proposals on my desk back at Starfleet within forty-eight hours. I'll review the specifics of your candidates' records, and consider other options as well. I'll render a decision as quickly as I can."

The meeting clearly over, Jellico began to head for the door, but then he slowed when he realized that Nechayev wasn't following him. He turned and looked at her questioningly.

"I need to talk with Captain Picard regarding another matter," she said. "If you wouldn't mind, Edward . . . ?"

Jellico tried to look indifferent as he shrugged and walked out, but Picard could tell that Jellico was annoyed. Then again, Riker had once observed that it was easy to tell when Jellico was annoyed: he was awake.

Nechayev turned to face Picard, her arms folded, and she said, "Regarding Calhoun . . ."

"I would hope, Admiral, that you haven't permitted Admiral Jellico's antipathy to prompt a hasty decision. . . ."

"Picard," Nechayev said slowly, "you have to understand that I'm about to tell you matters of a delicate nature."

The change in her tone puzzled Picard. "Delicate in what respect?"

She began to pace Picard's office. "There have been rumors, as Jellico mentioned, of Calhoun engaging in some shady dealings."

"As I said before, I would hope rumors wouldn't—"

"They're not rumors, Jean-Luc."

He raised an eyebrow. "Pardon?"

"Oh, the exact nature of Calhoun's activities may have been exaggerated in the retelling. These things always are. But Calhoun has engaged in some extremely questionable activities. I know because I assigned them."

"You—?"

"There are certain departments in Starfleet that prefer to keep a low profile, Captain. Offices that attend to matters which require a—how shall we say it—a subtle touch. Matters where general knowledge of Federation or Starfleet involvement would be counterproductive."

Picard couldn't quite believe it. "Are you saying that Calhoun has been acting as some sort of . . . of spy?"

" 'Spy' is such an ugly word, Captain," Nechayev said, sounding a bit amused. "We prefer the term 'specialist.' Mackenzie Calhoun has managed to establish a reputation for himself among certain quarters as a renegade Starfleet officer who will take on any assignment if the price is right. In doing so, he has both rooted out brewing problems and served our needs on certain occasions. You might say he is 'deep undercover.' "

"So he didn't leave Starfleet . . ."

"Oh, he left, all right. The incident involving the *Grissom* which prompted his departure was entirely genuine. But then he wound up getting himself into some trouble, and my office stepped in with a proposition that he couldn't exactly turn down. In short, we bailed him out of a situation from which he likely wouldn't have gotten out in one piece, and in return . . ."

"He's worked for you clandestinely. I see."

"It served both our needs, really. Mackenzie Calhoun is a man who needs challenges. He thrives on them."

"I know that all too well," acknowledged Picard.

"Well, we were able to provide him with that. It served the needs of all concerned."

"So what you're telling me is that Calhoun is out of the running. That you wish to reserve him for your . . . 'special needs.'"

Nechayev gazed out the window, her hands draped behind her back. "Not . . . necessarily," she said slowly. "I agree with you that Calhoun may be one of the best that the Academy ever turned out. Part of the reason for my recruiting him—under duress, I admit—was that I didn't want to lose him. I'm concerned that we may be on the verge of losing him now. He's been 'under' for too long, I think. Moving through disreputable, unsavory circles for so long that it's getting to him, bringing him down. Poisoning the essential goodness that is within him."

"He gazes into the abyss, and it gazes back."

"Exactly. For the purpose of achieving our own

ends, doing what needs to be done . . . I'm beginning to fear that we may have damaged the man's soul. If we don't do something about it soon, the damage may be irreparable. If I simply 'fire' him from the department, though . . . God knows what will happen to him. He needs a purpose in life, Picard. He needs Starfleet, even if he doesn't fully accept that."

"With that in mind, do you feel he's still capable of resuming a place of command in Starfleet?"

She turned and looked back at Picard. "At this moment, yes. This would be the ideal time. A year from now, perhaps even six months . . . it might be too late. He might be dead . . . or worse."

"Can you bring him in to Starfleet Headquarters? Talk with him?"

"I'm not entirely certain he would listen to me," she said. "Not about the subject of coming back to Starfleet. And as for bringing him in, well . . . I think, in this instance, it might be easier for the mountain to go to Mohammed . . . if you catch my drift."

IV.

KRASSUS STARED APPRAISINGLY at the cards in his hand, and then across the table at the insufferably smug face of the Xenexian who was his main opponent. Moments before, a Tellarite and an Andorian had also been in the game of Six-Card Warhoon, but they had folded their hands and were watching the duel of wills between Krassus and the Xenexian with some interest.

The Xenexian wasn't giving the slightest indication of what he had in his hand. His hair was long, and there was a fierce scar down the right side of his face. His purple eyes were dark as storm clouds, yet they looked at Krassus with a sort of bland disinterest. As if there weren't a fortune in latinum currently sitting in the pot.

Krassus knew little about the Xenexian beyond

that he apparently had some involvement in the slave trade. It was something that Krassus was comfortable with, what with slavery being his stock-in-trade as well. Krassus was an Orion, though, and had never had the opportunity to wander all that close to Xenexian space. But he'd heard through sources that Xenexians could be fairly tough customers, and this one seemed to be filling that bill admirably.

Krassus stroked his green chin thoughtfully. From nearby he heard a low chuckle. Zina was looking over his shoulder. "Stop breathing on me," he told her.

The scantily clad Orion slave girl took a step back, but she grinned in a manner that bordered on savage pleasure. Krassus had acquired Zina the previous year and had intended her for a quick resale, but he had taken a fancy to her. Even though he'd had a buyer lined up, he decided to keep her. The buyer had lodged a protest with Krassus. Krassus had, in response, lodged a dagger between the third and fourth ribs of the buyer, and that had put an end to the protest (and, for that matter, the buyer).

The reaction of the girl had not gone unnoticed by the Xenexian. "Seems to me like you've got a fairly good hand," said the Xenexian, "judging by your girlfriend's reaction. Perhaps I should fold right now."

In response, Krassus turned and cuffed Zina, knocking her back. She fell to the floor but landed like a panther, and she hissed fiercely at Krassus.

"Or perhaps," the Xenexian continued, "the two of you are working together to try and make me doubt myself. In which case . . ." He considered it, then nodded. "Yes. Yes, I believe that's probably it." He reached down into a case at his feet and pulled out two more bars of gold-pressed latinum, and dropped them onto the table. The table legs creaked slightly from the weight.

The card game had caught the attention by this point of all the rather seedy denizens of the equally seedy bar. Mojov Station was a way station convenient to several frontiers, a place where various types who might otherwise be questioned in more "civilized" establishments on more "civilized" worlds could come to relax, meet, greet, and try to parlay a few extra credits for themselves whenever possible.

Krassus looked at the bet, and felt the blood drain slightly from his face. "I can't cover that," he blustered.

"Seems to me like you're in trouble, then," replied the Xenexian.

Krassus' eyes flickered from his hand (which was a very solid one) to the bet on the table, and his greed was becoming overwhelming . . . to say nothing of his pride over the thought of losing to this pasty-faced Xenexian. Then his eyes caught Zina and he looked back at the Xenexian. "How about her?"

Zina was shocked to hear herself being put up as a

bet, but the Xenexian didn't seem the least bit surprised. It was as if he was expecting it. "She worth two bars of latinum? I don't think so."

"What she can provide in straight-up resale would be far less. What Zina can provide in the way of . . . physical gratification . . . she's worth ten times that. I speak from personal experience." Krassus chortled.

"Krassus!" she snarled.

The Xenexian regarded her thoughtfully. "If I won you, Zina . . . would you try to kill me as payback? Or would you show gratitude for one who would treat you far better than a man who'd put you up for a stake in a game of Six-Card Warhoon?"

Zina appeared to consider the point. Then a look of contempt crossed her face as she said to the Xenexian, "Clearly I have no more reason to be loyal to Krassus than he has to be loyal to me. Do what you will, Xenexian . . . and if it falls your way, I'll do what you will, as well."

"Fair enough," said the Xenexian. "It's a bet, Orion."

"Excellent!" crowed Krassus. "We finally have a game for true men, Xenexian! And now let us see which of us is the better!"

The back rooms in the bar were available for rent for just this sort of occasion, as the Xenexian strode into the room, pivoting quickly on his heel to make sure that the Orion girl wasn't behind his back. Zina stood framed into the door, grinning ferally, her eyes sparkling. The room wasn't elaborately furnished; then again, the sturdy bed in the corner wasn't really much more than the room really required.

"I guess Krassus learned who was the better," she purred. "The great fool."

"More fool he," agreed the Xenexian.

"And what shall I call you?" She slinked across the floor, her hips swaying, the scraps of cloth that served as her clothing barely clinging to her.

"Mac," he said.

"And will you sell me, Mac? You own me now. Will you sell me, or keep me?"

"I thought I'd reserve judgment on that," said Mac.

"Until when?"

"An hour or two from now."

She sprang toward him, and his first reflex was to try and shove her away. But she wrapped herself around him in a rather unthreatening manner, her arms behind his back, her legs straddling his hips. "Merely an hour?" she said challengingly with a raised brow. "I think we can make up your mind faster than that."

And then her lips were against his, hungrily, and it seemed as if she weren't a woman so much as she was a force of nature. She practically stole Mac's breath away as she pulled at his clothing, trying to yank his loose shirt off him. He staggered back toward the bed, hit the mattress, and fell back onto it. She literally ripped off his shirt and started to do things down his bare chest.

He pulled her up to face him, looked into her eyes, and felt as if he were being sucked into a maelstrom. Her lips were drawn back, her teeth glittering and white, and he rolled her over so that he was atop her. Somewhere in all of that her clothes fell away, his chest pressed against her, and the heat was over-whelming. Her hands reached below his waist as his own arms extended up toward the pillow that lay at the far end of the bed.

The door to the room opened in complete silence. The Xenexian named Mac did not see Krassus enter, moving with stealth that seemed unnatural in one so large. Zina spotted him, though, but she said nothing . . . merely hissed more loudly to cover his entrance. Krassus carried a large knife, which glit-tered in the dim lighting of the room. He kept it highly polished, incredibly sharp. Keeping it clean was something of a challenge considering the num-ber of times that he had shed blood with it.

He took two quick, silent steps and was across the room, the knife brought up over his head as he prepared to bring it slamming down. The Xenexian was oblivious, his back glistening with sweat, his right hand under the pillow. . . .

And suddenly there was a shriek of energy which tore through the pillow, blasting it apart, slicing through the air, slicing through Krassus. The energy bolt hit him dead square in the stomach, knocking him off his feet. He dropped the knife and, at that same instant, Mac suddenly arched his back and shoved Zina out from under him. She hit the floor, stunned and confused, as Mac snagged the falling knife from midair with his left hand. In his right hand he was holding the blaster he'd stashed under the pillow.

All of this happened before Krassus had even had time to hit the floor. The momentum of the energy bolt had slammed him back against the door, and he now slid to the floor with obvious confusion in his eyes.

Mac eased himself off the bed. From the floor, Zina looked at the fallen Krassus in shock and then back at the Xenexian. "You . . . you shot him . . . and you . . . you didn't even see him . . ."

"Practice," Mac said evenly. His voice, his demeanor, seemed to have changed. He seemed more in command, more formidable than before. If Zina were a fanciful type, she would have imagined that thunderclouds were massing over his head.

He walked slowly over toward Krassus, who was lying on the floor, clutching his belly. Blood was fountaining out, and Krassus was clutching things that he didn't even want to think about touching, trying to shove them back into his body. Mac crouched down, and his eyes were dead and cold. "Gut shot," he said, almost as if commiserating. "Takes a while to die of those. Painful as hell. And the damage is too extreme for any nearby med facility. You're dead. Of course"—he twirled the knife in his hand with surprising expertise; it seemed to come alive in his long fingers—"if you wish, I can end it for you faster."

"You . . . you bastard . . ." stammered out Krassus.

Mac nodded slowly. "Yes. I imagine so. But even bastards have friends. I've had a few, including one who saved my life once. His name was Barsamis. Name seem familiar?" At first Krassus shook his head, and then his eyes went wide in realization. "Ah. You remember him. Good," said Mac. "Barsamis had his faults, certainly. Something of a lowlife, really. But, as I said, he saved my life on one occasion, and that made me beholden to him. I owed him, and then some Orion slave trader violated an agreement and wound up killing him. Shoved a knife between his ribs." He looked speculatively at the blade in his hand. "This one, perhaps? Was this the knife?"

Wordlessly, Krassus nodded.

"Well, then," said Mac. "I'd say this falls into the realm of poetic justice, wouldn't you?"

And suddenly the warning tingled in the base of Mac's skull.

There was nothing psychic about the knack he had, nor anything mystical. The Xenexian simply had a knack for knowing when danger was imminent, and was able to react with speed and aim that seemed—to anyone else—supernatural. In the case of Krassus, of course, it had been easy. He'd been expecting just such a tactic as Krassus had pulled, and was prepared for it.

The attack of the Orion girl, Zina, on the other hand, was a bit more ill timed.

Zina leaped at him, and Mac—still from a crouched position—slammed out with his right foot. It caught Zina squarely in the gut while she was still in midair and sent her falling to the floor. It did not, however, slow her down significantly. With an animal roar she was upon him, her fingers outstretched, her nails bared.

And out of the corner of his eye, Mac saw Krassus starting to reach into the folds of his shirt. It was possible that Krassus was simply trying to stop the bleeding. On the other hand, it was also possible that he was about to pull a weapon.

Mac took no chance. He yanked the blaster from his belt and swung it around with his left hand, the barrel hitting the Orion girl full in the face. He heard a crack which told him that he'd likely broken her lower jaw as she went down, screeching. His right hand, meantime, swept in an arc, slicing through Krassus's throat, severing his vocal cords, cutting through major arteries. Dark blood poured out from Krassus's throat and he slumped back, his eyes rolling up into the top of his head.

Mac scrambled to his feet as Zina backed against the far wall. There was the look of the wild, wounded animal in her face. Her damaged jaw fed pain into her that fueled her rage, and Mac brought the blaster up and even with her. "This has one setting, and it's a fatal one," Mac warned her. "I don't want to have to kill you . . . but I will."

Zina, with a bestial roar, leaped at him.

And a split second before he could squeeze the trigger, he sensed someone else behind him, but he couldn't fire in two directions at the same time. And then there was a blast from behind him, accompanied by the familiar whine of a phaser. The stun blast struck Zina and flipped her backward over the bed. She hit the floor and lay there, unmoving.

Mac spun, his blaster still leveled since he had no idea what to expect. But even if he had known . . . he would still have been surprised.

"I'll be damned," he said.

Jean-Luc Picard stood in the doorway, his phaser in his hand. He was dressed in civilian clothes of dark black. He was looking down at the bloody corpse of Krassus, and then slowly he shifted his gaze to Mac. "What the hell happened in here? Tell me it was self-defense."

"It was self-defense."

"Would you lie if it were otherwise?"

Calhoun's eyes flashed. "To others, yes. To you, no." He paused. "Did you come in a ship?"

"Of course."

"Let's get in it and I'll tell you." He started for the door, then paused and said, "Leave first. I'll follow a minute or so later. I don't want to be seen with you."

"Why not?"

"You know what you look like, Picard?"

Despite the goriness of the situation, the violence

that had infested the room mere moments before, Picard couldn't help but smile inwardly. Reverence was never one of Mackenzie Calhoun's strong suits. "What do I look like, Calhoun?"

"You look like a Starfleet officer dressed in civilian clothes. If I'm spotted with you, I'll be ruining my reputation."

As the runabout hurtled away from Mojov Station, Picard turned from the controls to study Calhoun's face. He felt as if he were trying to find, somewhere within, the young man he had met twenty years ago. Calhoun, for his part, was calmly wiping away the last traces of Krassus' blood from his hands.

"You had to kill him, didn't you," Picard asked after a time.

Calhoun looked up. "Yes. It was self-defense."

"That's how you arranged it. You allowed yourself to be pulled into a situation where you knew that you would be attacked . . . and then could defend yourself with lethal force."

Calhoun put down the towel he was using to dry himself. "He killed a man to whom I owed my life," he said. "Honor demanded that the score be evened. But I'm not an assassin. I couldn't just walk in and kill him."

"You're splitting hairs, M'k'n'zy."

"At least, unlike you, I still have hairs to split," replied Calhoun with a lopsided grin. He sat back. "Gods . . . 'M'k'n'zy.' It's been ages since I went by that. Hurt my ears to listen to people muck up the gutturals. Closest Terran tongues came was 'Mackenzie.'"

"Yes, I know. You officially changed your name on your records. M'k'n'zy of Calhoun became Mackenzie Calhoun."

"'Mac,' to my friends." He eyed Picard with open curiosity. "Do you fall into that category, Picard?"

"I would like to think so." He paused. "You're trying to drag me off topic, which is something in which you've often excelled. The point is . . . if you have a grievance, you could have . . ."

"Could have what? Arrested him? Tried to bring him in for Federation justice? Picard," and he leaned forward, staring out into space, "it's different when you're out there. When you're on your own. When you don't have the power of the Federation at your beck and call. I work best outside the system, Picard . . . and since you've made a surprise visit, I take it you're aware of just how outside the system I am."

"And did it bring you personal satisfaction? Killing that Orion?"

He blew air impatiently between his lips. "Yes. Is that what you want to hear, Picard? Yes, it did." He sat there for a moment and then turned to gaze steadily at Picard. And in that dark stare, Picard saw a hint, just a hint, of a soul that had terrified armed men twenty years ago. Saw the fires that burned within Calhoun. "Don't you get it, Picard? I'm a savage. I always have been. I've created this . . . this

cloak of civilization that I wrap around myself as
need be. But I've kept this to remind me." He ran a
finger down the scar on his face. "As much as I've
tried to leave behind my roots, I've still felt it
necessary to keep this with me so I never forget."

"Calhoun . . . Mac . . ."

"Do you know why I did it, Picard?"

"You told me. You killed him because—"

"Not that." He waved dismissively as if the Orion
were unimportant. "Why I followed your sugges-
tions. Why, when you eventually told me you
thought I was destined for greatness. I—in my
naïveté—believed you."

"You've never gone into specifics. I thought—"

"I had a vision of you, Picard. As absurd as it
sounds . . . before we met. I had a vision of you. I
believed that you would be important in my life."

"A vision? You mean a dream?"

"I mean I saw you as clearly, as plainly, as I see
you here and now. I saw you and . . ." His voice
trailed off.

"And—?"

"And . . . someone else. Someone with whom I
was . . . involved. We kept our affair rather dis-
creet."

"It did not end well, I take it."

"Nothing ends well, Picard. Happy endings are an
invention of fantasists and fools."

"Oh, stop it!" Picard said so sharply that it caught
Calhoun's attention. "Self-pity does not become
you. It doesn't become anyone in Starfleet."

Calhoun got up and strode toward the back of the runabout. Setting the computer on autoguide, Picard followed him. Calhoun turned and leaned against the back wall, facing Picard.

"You should never have resigned, Mac. That's the simple fact of the matter. I know you blamed yourself for what happened on your previous assignment, the *Grissom.*"

"Don't bring it up."

"But Starfleet cleared you. . . ."

"I said don't bring it up!" said Calhoun furiously. The scar seemed to stand out against his face and, bubbling with anger, he shoved Picard out of the way as he started to head back to the helm of the runabout.

And to Calhoun's astonishment, Picard grabbed Calhoun by the wrist and swung him back around. Calhoun banged into the wall and, as much as from surprise as anything else, slid to the ground. He looked up at Picard in astonishment. "Trying your hand at savagery yourself, Picard?" he asked.

Picard stabbed a finger at him. "Dammit, Calhoun, I believed in you! I looked into your eyes twenty years ago and I saw greatness! Greatness that did not deserve to be confined on Xenex."

"You should have left me the hell alone. Just as you should now."

"That is not an option. You're a Starfleet officer. No matter what you are now . . . that is what you will always be. You cannot turn away from that. You have a *destiny*. Don't you dare let it slide away. Now get up. Get up, if you're a man."

There was something about the words . . . something that stirred in Calhoun's memory. He automatically relegated what Picard was saying now—something about the Thallonians—to some dim and less important portion of his mind as he tried to dredge up the phrasing.

". . . and it is my belief that no one could be more suited—" Picard was saying.

"Jean-Luc, please, just . . . give me a moment," and the sincerity in Calhoun's tone stopped Picard cold. Calhoun pulled himself to standing and he was eye-to-eye with Picard. He was lost in thought, and Picard—sensing something was up—said nothing. Then Calhoun snapped his fingers. "Of course. You said that to me then. Gods, I haven't thought about it in years. . . ."

"I said what?"

"About my being a Starfleet officer. About destiny."

Suddenly looking much older, Calhoun walked across the runabout and dropped back into the helm chair. "That's the problem, Picard. That's always been the problem. I could see the future so clearly, even when I was a young man. I saw my people free, and it was so clear, so pure a vision, that I couldn't help but believe that I was destined to bring them to that freedom. And then I saw you . . . don't ask me how. And again I felt destiny tapping me on the shoulder, pointing me, guiding me. I guess . . . I had it easy."

"Easy?" Picard looked stunned. "You had an upbringing more brutal than anyone who wasn't raised a Klingon. Easy, you say?"

"Yes, easy. Because I never doubted myself, Picard. Not ever. I never doubted that I was destined for something. And I . . ." he smiled grimly. "I never lost. Oh, I had setbacks. I had obstacles thrown in my way. But in the end, I always triumphed. Moreover, I knew I would. And when I worked my way up to first officer on the *Grissom* . . ." He shooked his head. "Dammit, Jean-Luc, no one guides a planet to freedom unless he feels that he was born to win. That feeling never left me."

"Until the *Grissom* disaster."

"Yes."

Picard sighed deeply. "Mac . . . I've been where you are now. I've suffered . . . personal disaster. Indignities. Torment, psychological and physical. And I'd be lying if I said there weren't times I nearly walked away from it all. When my body, my soul screamed, 'Enough. Enough.' But destiny doesn't simply call to Xenexian rebel leaders, Mackenzie. In a way, it calls to anyone who aspires to command of a starship."

"Anyone such as you," said Calhoun.

"And you. It called to you once, and it summons you now. You cannot, you must not, turn a deaf ear."

Calhoun shook his head. "It's crazy. You're not actually suggesting I get back on the bridge of a starship, are you?"

"That is exactly what I am suggesting. In fact, that's what I recommended, both to Admiral Nechayev and Admiral Jellico."

"Jellico?" Calhoun looked up and made no effort to hide his disdain. "He's an admiral now? Good lord, Jean-Luc, you want me to re-up with an organization so blind to talent that it would elevate someone like Jellico?"

"Jellico accomplishes that which he is assigned," Picard replied evenly. "We all of us work to the limits of our individual gifts. Except for a handful of us who walk away from those gifts."

"This is guilt. You're trying to guilt me."

"I'm trying to remind you that you're capable of greater things than skulking around the galaxy, accomplishing clandestine missions. Yes, you're doing the jobs assigned you. I take nothing away from your small achievements. But a Mackenzie Calhoun is not meant for small achievements. That is a waste of potential." He leaned forward, rested a hand on Calhoun's arm. "Twenty years ago I met a young man with more raw talent than any I'd ever encountered before . . . and quite possibly since. That talent has been shaped and honed and focused. Your service record was exemplary, and you cannot—must not—allow what happened with the *Grissom* to destroy you. Think of it this way: The *Grissom* disaster, and the subsequent court-martial . . . your resignation, your guilt . . . these are scars which you carry on the inside. But they are merely scars, not mortal wounds, and you must use them to propel you forward as much as the scar you carry on the outside does. The fact is, there is a starship that needs a captain, and a mission that would seem to call for your . . . particular talents. Do not let Starfleet, or yourself, down."

Calhoun leaned back in his chair, stroked his chin thoughtfully, and gazed out once more at the passing stars. Picard wondered what was going through his head.

He was a savage at heart, that much Picard knew. In some ways, he reminded Picard of Worf. But there were differences, though. Worf always seemed about as relaxed as a dormant volcano. His ferocity was a perpetual and prominent part of his nature. But Calhoun had gone much further. He had virtually created an entire persona for himself. As he'd said himself, a sort of cloak that he could wrap around himself, and use to keep the world at bay and his inward, tempestuous nature away from the world. As a consequence, he was uniquely focused, uniquely adept at problem solving, and one of the most dedicated individuals Picard had ever encountered.

What was he thinking? What great moral issues was he considering as he contemplated the thought of reentering Starfleet openly, to pursue his first, best destiny? What soul-searching, gut-wrenching contemplation was—?

Calhoun looked at Picard with a clear, mischievous air. "If I take command of a starship, Jellico will have a fit, won't he."

Picard considered the matter. "Yes. He probably will."

Calhoun leaned forward, and there was a sparkle of sadistic amusement in his eye. "So tell me about this ship you want to put me on. . . ."

V.

THE LIGHT WAS BLINKING on Soleta's computer when she entered her apartment. As she removed her jacket, she looked at the flashing light with a distant curiosity. Outside it appeared that a storm front was moving in. It was clearly visible hanging in the distance over Starfleet Academy. It had already obscured her normally excellent view of the Golden Gate Bridge.

Soleta shrugged off her jacket and hung it carefully in her closet. She made several quick mental notes regarding lesson plans for tomorrow's class, and—since she was eminently capable of accomplishing more than one task at a time—she said briskly. "Computer. Messages."

"Two messages," replied the computer. "Playing first message."

The screen wavered for a moment, and then the image of Commander Seth Goddard from Starfleet Central appeared. His hair graying at the temples, Goddard was all business. "Lieutenant Soleta, this message has a callback command built in. Wait for live transmission, please."

Soleta sat down in front of the screen, folding her hands neatly in front of her. She wondered what Central could possibly want with her. She'd been fairly low-profile since taking on the teaching duties at Starfleet Academy. It was not precisely the life that she had anticipated for herself, but it was one that gave her satisfaction. Her journey of personal discovery as she endeavored to deal with her mixed heritage had been a long and rocky one. But that was far behind her now. She was at peace with herself.

At least, she liked to tell herself that.

The screen flickered to life and Goddard's image appeared on it. 'Ah. Lieutenant. I appreciate your prompt response."

"How may I help you, sir?"

"You can help me by packing."

She looked at him blankly. " 'Packing,' sir? I don't . . . ?"

"You're being reactivated, Lieutenant. You're shipping out next week on the *Excalibur*."

"Sir . . . no," she said with as much surprise as she ever allowed herself. "I do not . . . I am not seeking a shipboard position. I had thought that was clear to all concerned. That my place was here on Earth."

"It's called 'Starfleet,' Lieutenant, not 'Earthfleet.' I'm afraid you can't hide here forever."

"With all respect, sir, I am not hiding. I am doing a job, and a valuable one at that."

"You're doing a job that can be filled by at least a hundred people currently in the pipeline, all equally as capable as you. You're needed on the *Excalibur* as science officer, and you are the person singly suited to the job. Besides, you came highly recommended."

"Science officer . . . ? Recommended . . . ?" She was becoming frustrated by her communication skills, or apparent sudden lack thereof. "Recommended by whom?"

"Ambassador Spock."

If she had not become as skilled as she was at covering her surprise, she would have had to pick up her jaw off the ground in front of her. "Ambassador . . . Spock."

"I presume the name is familiar to you."

"Oh yes. Most familiar. And we have met. But I am still unclear as to . . . as to why he would recommend me for anything. Science officer, sir?"

"That's correct, Lieutenant."

"On the *Excalibur.*" Despite her hesitation, she was annoyed to find a tingle of anticipation. It wasn't as if they had abruptly decided to stick her on a science vessel and send her into the middle of nowhere. This was the *Excalibur,* a starship with a long and illustrious history. But then she tried, with determination, to shake off her momentary anticipation of the new assignment. "But sir, I still do not understand why, of all individuals, I am being assigned to this vessel. It has been three years, five months, and eighteen days since I logged any space time at all."

"You'll get your space legs back in no time," Goddard told her. "But you're probably wondering why we've zeroed in on you. Why the ambassador singled you out."

"Yes, sir, I believe I have asked that repeatedly."

The faint tone of criticism didn't appear to register on him. "The *Excalibur* is going to have a very specific assignment, Lieutenant. Sector 221-G."

Soleta did not even have to search her memory to pull that very familiar number up. "Thallonian space," she said slowly.

"That's right, Lieutenant."

"I had heard that there were difficulties. There were stories of refugees . . . civil war . . ."

"All that and more. And we're sending the *Excalibur* into the heart of it. It's going to be one hell of an adventure. I wish I could go with you."

"If the commander wishes. I would most happily step aside from my new post in deference to his own desires."

"Very funny, Lieutenant," said Goddard. "Let's not forget, you're still in Starfleet. The powers that be feel that, considering you're one of a bare handful of people who spent any time there, that your presence is essential."

Her instinct was to protest, to go over Goddard's head. Spock's recommendation aside, she was happy teaching. She had no desire to thrust herself once more into the rigors and dangers of space.

But still . . .

She couldn't help but feel that the mystery of Thallon remained an open door to her. There was something about that planet, something that intrigued her, and she'd never been able to investigate it. It had nagged at the back of her mind on and off for years, and the pronouncement from the commander catapulted it straight to the forefront.

"Very well, sir. I'll be ready."

"Good. Goddard out."

His image vanished, to be replaced by a blank screen and the computer voice saying, "Second message. Visual only."

She stared at the screen in confusion. There was just blackness; surely it was a mistake. But then, slowly, letters began to appear on the screen. Two words formed.

And the words were, *Don't move.*

"Don't move?" said Soleta in confusion. "What kind of message is that?"

And then she felt the blunt end of some sort of blaster weapon lodge itself securely in her neck. She couldn't believe it. Whoever was behind her, either they had entered the apartment while she was speaking to Goddard, or else they had actually been present the entire time and Soleta—despite her keen hearing—had been utterly oblivious.

"It is the kind of message," a soft but threatening voice said, "that you should pay attention to, if you know what is best for you. Now . . . you shall do exactly what I say . . . and may God help you if you do not, because no one else will be able to help you. That, I can assure you."

To Be Continued

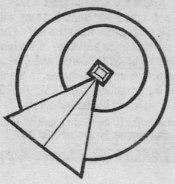

SPECIAL
Limited Edition

STAR TREK®
VULCAN'S FORGE

BOOKPLATE OFFER!

Fill out the coupon below and send it, along with the proof of purchase (the clipped corner from the inside back jacket flap that shows the product price and title) of the hardcover edition of *STAR TREK: VULCAN'S FORGE* and the cash register receipt with the purchase price circled, to the address below and receive an autographed *VULCAN'S FORGE* bookplate signed by the authors!

(Offer good only in the United States and while supplies last; offer expires December 31st, 1997.)

STAR TREK: VULCAN'S FORGE Special Bookplate Offer

Name_____

Address_____Apt #_____

City_____ State____Zip_____

Mail this completed form to:
STAR TREK: VULCAN'S FORGE Bookplate Offer,
P.O. Box 9266 (Dept. 10) Bridgeport, NJ 08014-9266

Intrepid II and Obsidian,
Day 4, Fifth Week, Month of the Raging *Durak*,
Year 2296

Lieutenant Duchamps, staring at the sight of Obsidian growing ever larger in the viewscreen, pursed his lips in a silent whistle. "Would you look at that. . . ."

Captain Spock, who had been studying the viewscreen as well, glanced quickly at the helmsman. "Lieutenant?"

Duchamps, predictably, went back into too-formal mode at this sudden attention. "The surface of Obsidian, sir. I was thinking how well-named it is, sir. All those sheets of that black volcanic glass glittering in the sun. Sir."

"That black volcanic glass is, indeed, what constitutes the substance known as obsidian," Spock observed, though only someone extremely familiar with Vulcans—James Kirk, for instance—could have read any dry humor into his matter-of-fact voice. Getting to his feet, Spock added to Uhura, "I am leaving for the transporter room, Commander. You have the conn."

"Yes, sir."

He waited to see her seated in the command chair, knowing how important this new role was to her, then acknowledged Uhura's right to be there with the smallest of nods. She solemnly nodded back, aware that he had just offered her silent congratulations. But Uhura being Uhura, she added in quick mischief, "Now, don't forget to write!"

After so many years among humans, Spock knew perfectly well that this was meant as a good-natured, tongue-in-cheek farewell, but he obligingly retorted, "I see no reason why I should utilize so inappropriate a means of communication," and was secretly gratified to see Uhura's grin.

He was less gratified at the gasps of shock from the rest of the bridge crew. Did they not see the witticism as such? Or were they shocked that Uhura could dare be so familiar? Spock firmly blocked a twinge of very illogical nostalgia; illogical, he told himself, because the past was exactly that.

McCoy was waiting for him, for once silent on the subject of "having my molecules scattered all over Creation." With the doctor were several members of Security and a few specialists, such as the friendly, sensible Lieutenant Clayton, an agronomist, and the efficient young Lieutenant Diver, a geologist so new to Starfleet that her insignia still looked like they'd just come out of the box. Various other engineering and medical personnel would be following later. The heaviest of the doctor's supplies had already been beamed down with other equipment, but he stubbornly clung to the medical satchel—his "little black bag," as McCoy so anachronistically called it—slung over his shoulder.

"I decided to go," he told Spock unnecessarily. "That outrageously high rate of skin cancer and lethal mutations makes it a fascinating place."

That seemingly pure-science air, Spock mused, fooled no one. No doctor worthy of the title could turn away from so many hurting people.

"Besides," McCoy added acerbically, "someone's got to make sure you all wear your sunhats."

"Indeed. Energize," Spock commanded, and . . .

. . . was elsewhere, from the unpleasantly cool, relatively dim ship—cool and dim to Vulcan senses, at any rate—to the dazzlingly bright light and welcoming heat of Obsidian. The veils instantly slid down over Spock's eyes, then up again as his desert-born vision adapted, while the humans hastily adjusted their sun visors. He glanced about at this new world, seeing a flat, gravelly surface, tan-brown-gray stretching to the horizon of jagged, clearly volcanic peaks. A hot wind teased grit and sand into miniature spirals, and the sun glinted off shards of the black volcanic glass that had given this world its Federation name.

"Picturesque," someone commented wryly, but Spock ignored that. Humans, he knew, used sarcasm to cover uneasiness. Or perhaps it was discomfort; perhaps they felt the higher level of ionization in the air as he did, prickling at their skin.

No matter. One accepted what could not be changed. They had, at David Rabin's request, beamed down to these coordinates a distance away from the city: "The locals are uneasy enough as it is without a sudden 'invasion' in their midst."

Logical. And there was the Federation detail he had been told to expect, at its head a sturdy, familiar figure: David Rabin. He stepped forward, clad in a standard Federation hot-weather outfit save for his decidedly non-standard-issue headgear of some loose, flowing material caught by a circle of corded rope. Sensible, Spock thought, to adapt what was clearly an effective local solution to the problem of sunstroke.

"Rabin of Arabia," McCoy muttered, but Spock let that pass. Captain Rabin, grinning widely, was offering him the split-fingered Vulcan Greeting of the Raised Hand and saying, "Live long and prosper."

There could be no response but one. Spock returned the salutation and replied simply, "Shalom."

This time McCoy had nothing to say.

It was only a short drive to the outpost. "Solar-powered vehicles, of course," Rabin noted. "No shortage of solar power on this world! The locals don't really mind our getting around like this as long as we don't bring any vehicles into Kalara or frighten the *chuchaki*—those cameloid critters over there."

Spock forbore to criticize the taxonomy.

Kalara, he mused, looked very much the standard desert city to be found on many low-tech, and some high-tech, worlds. Mud brick really was the most practical organic building material, and thick walls and high windows provided quite efficient passive air cooling. Kalara was, of course, an oasis town; he didn't need to see the oasis to extrapolate that conclusion. No desert city came into being without a steady, reliable source of water and, therefore, a steady, reliable source of food. Spock noted the tips of some feathery green branches peeking over the high walls and nodded. Good planning for both economic and safety reasons to have some of that reliable water source be within the walls. Add to that the vast underground network of irrigation canals and wells, and these people were clearly doing a clever job of exploiting their meager resources.

Or would be, were it not for that treacherous sun.

And, judging from what Rabin had already warned, for that all too common problem in times of crisis: fanaticism.

It is illogical, he thought, for any one person or persons to claim to know a One True Path to enlightenment. And I must, he added honestly, include my own distant ancestors in that thought.

And, he reluctantly added, some Vulcans not so far removed in time.

"What's *that?*" McCoy exclaimed suddenly. "Hebrew graffiti?"

"Deuteronomy," Rabin replied succinctly, adding, "We're home, everybody."

They left the vehicles and entered the Federation outpost, and in the process made a jarring jump from timelessness to gleaming modernity. Spock paused only an instant at the shock of what to him was a wall of unwelcome coolness; around him, the humans were all breathing sighs of relief. McCoy put down his shoulder pack with a grunt. "Hot as Vulcan out there."

"Just about," Rabin agreed cheerfully, pulling off his native headgear. "And if you think this is bad, wait till Obsidian's summer. This sun, good old unstable Loki, will kill you quite efficiently.

"Please, everyone, relax for a bit. Drink something even if you don't feel thirsty. It's ridiculously easy to dehydrate here, especially when none of you are desert acclimated. Or rather," he added before Spock could comment, "when even the desert-born among you haven't been *in* any deserts for a while. While you're resting, I'll fill you in on what's been happening here."

Quickly and efficiently, Rabin set out the various problems—the failed hydroponics program, the beetles, the mysterious fires and spoiled supply dumps. When he was finished, Spock noted, "One, two or even three incidents might be considered no more than unpleasant coincidence. But taken as a whole, this series of incidents can logically only add up to deliberate sabotage."

"Which is what I was thinking," Rabin agreed. "'One's accident, two's coincidence, three's enemy action,' or however the quote goes. The trouble is: Who *is* the enemy? Or rather, which one?"

Spock raised an eyebrow ever so slightly. "These are, if the records are indeed correct, a desert people with a relatively low level of technology."

"They are that. And before you ask, no, there's absolutely no trace of Romulan or any other off-world involvement."

"Then we need ask: Who of this world would have sufficient organization and initiative to work such an elaborate scheme of destruction?"

The human sighed. "Who, indeed? We've got a good many local dissidents; we both know how many nonconformists a desert can breed. But none of the local brand of agitators could ever band together long enough to mount a definite threat. They hate each other as much or maybe even more than they hate us."

"And in the desert?"

"Ah, Spock, old buddy, just how much manpower do you think I have? Much as I'd love to up and search all that vastness—"

"It would mean leaving the outpost unguarded. I understand."

"Besides," Rabin added thoughtfully, "I can't believe that any of the desert people, even the 'wild nomads,' as the folks in Kalara call the deep-desert tribes, would do anything to destroy precious resources, even those from off-world. They might destroy *us,* but not food or water."

"Logic," Spock retorted, "requires that someone is working this harm. Whether you find the subject pleasant or not, *someone* is 'poisoning the wells.' "

"Excuse me, sir," Lieutenant Clayton said, "but wouldn't it be relatively simple for the *Intrepid* to do a scan of the entire planet?"

"It could—"

"But that," Rabin cut in, "wouldn't work. The trouble is those 'wild nomads' are a pain in the . . . well, they're a nuisance to find by scanning because they tend to hide out against solar flares. And where they hide is in hollows shielded by rock that's difficult or downright impossible for scanners to penetrate. We have no idea how many nomads are out there, nor do the city folk. Oh, and if that wasn't enough," he added wryly, "the high level of ionization in the atmosphere, thank you very much Loki, provides a high amount of static to signal."

Spock moved to the banks of equipment set up to measure ionization, quickly scanning the data. "The levels do fluctuate within the percentages of possibility. A successful scan is unlikely but not improbable during the lower ranges of the scale. We will attempt one. I have a science officer who will regard this as a personal challenge." As do I, he added silently. A Vulcan could, after all, assemble the data far more swiftly than a human who— No. McCoy had quite wisely warned him against "micromanaging." He was not what he had been, Spock reminded himself severely. And only an emotional being longed for what had been and was no more.

Look for STAR TREK Fiction from Pocket Books

Star Trek®: The Original Series

Star Trek: Deep Space Nine®

Star Trek®: Voyager™

Flashback • Diane Carey
The Black Shore • Greg Cox
Mosaic • Jeri Taylor

Star Trek®: New Frontier